Curse Me Under the Mistletoe

A HEX ON ME MYSTERY
BOOK FIVE

KENNEDY LAYNE

CURSE ME UNDER THE MISTLETOE

DEDICATION

Jeffrey—You're the reason I believe in miracles every single day!

Cole—Never forget that miracles do happen!

Curses and kisses are stirring up a cloud of fresh snowflakes this holiday season in the latest installment in the Hex on Me Mysteries by USA Today Bestselling Author Kennedy Layne…

Delicious peppermint candy canes, a mug of creamy hot chocolate, and a deadly curse all seem to be connected in the next mystery that Lou and the gang unravel just in time for the winter solstice. Not for the first time, another one of Lou's premonitions ends up with a dead body. This time, there seems to be a seasonal twist…in the form of a very special type of mistletoe.

Grab your earmuffs and scarves if you want to help Lou and the gang solve this latest whodunit in a magical winter wonderland this holiday season!

Chapter One

THERE WAS SOMETHING about a winter wonderland during the holiday season that was always so magical, it could actually make one believe in Christmas miracles. Chestnuts roasting over an open fire might have been the opening line of a very popular song back in the day, but the actual endeavor was something of a tradition that I'd come to miss over the years. Add in steamy mugs of creamy hot chocolate with an abundance of melting marshmallows dissolving near the brim, and it was the perfect way to spend an evening a week before Christmas.

"That's somewhat debatable. Did you notice that the inside of the RV now reeks of that peppermint candle that Piper saw fit to ignite?" Orwin asked with a grimace, startling me out of my reverie. He was casually shuffling the cast iron skillet back and forth over the fire, waiting for the delicious chestnuts to darken to perfection. He was only roasting the special treat because I'd mentioned a week ago that it had been a fond memory from my childhood. "I never did like candy canes much, and now the entire place is one big holiday treat. I think it's due to the time my brother iced my sugar cookies with toothpaste as a joke. It literally took hours to get that taste out of my mouth. I highly doubt swallowing that much toothpaste was good for a growing boy. Anyway, if that wasn't bad enough, I'm running on about three hours of sleep between decorating and researching potential leads. We have enough strands of lights on and in the RV for us to be seen from the International Space Station. It's a good thing we're on shore power. The generator might not handle the load as we've overdone it a bit."

I never would have considered you to be a Grinch, Mr. Cornelia. Siblings will be siblings, after all. Although, I now understand why there is watermelon-flavored toothpaste in the bathroom. I daresay your bad mood is due to being confirmed as a distant relative of an immortal Lich. What's the old saying? You can't choose your family, or some such odd American colloquialism. Really, you're just going to give yourself the collywobbles if you continue to focus on something so insignificant.

That English-accented voice belongs to Pearl Pippa Allifair, who just so happens to be a familiar attuned to our good friend Piper Allifair and our resident etiquette guru. She didn't fool me in the least, though. She was very well-acquainted with every old adage to have ever been uttered in the past two thousand years while she'd been roaming this earth, and she'd been doing her best to quell Orwin's revulsion upon discovering his immortal connection as a long-lost blood relative to the oldest living witch in history.

I don't believe I'm doing a good enough job, Miss Lilura.

Speaking of witches, my name is Tempest Darcinean Lilura. Lou to my friends.

Sadly, I had been the unfortunate recipient of said Lich's wrath, and let me tell you that it hadn't been even remotely been a blessing in disguise. It was a flat-out hex. The result had been totally ironic, too—I'd ended up a cursed witch, of all things. Who would have ever thought that was even possible?

You'd be surprised at what could possibly occur in the supernatural realm, Miss Lilura. I've been around to witness rather spectacular situations that human beings are very eager to dismiss.

As I was saying, I'd actually been a psychology professor at a small community college in the state of Washington in my recent past. I'd had a fantastic life, good friends, and a great apartment until that fateful day when I was hexed by the vilest creature on the face of this planet. A remnant of centuries past—evil incarnate.

You see, Ammeline Letty Romilda had been believed to be nothing more than an urban legend told in the form of a bedtime story to scare children into their best behavior to avoid her wrath. I recalled childhood memories of hearing different tales on the same subject time and time again. Never in my life would I have ever imagined that she was a real entity.

A spot of warm cream always helps to keep my nightmares away, Miss Lilura. It might work for you or our friend, Mr. Cornelia.

"Well, I didn't know that I was Ammeline's great, great, great, great-nephew, either," Orwin responded in disgust, being close enough to read my mind, much like Pearl. He'd been given the gift of telepathy through his bloodline, though he did have to be within six feet of a person to hear his or her thoughts. He pushed up his black-rimmed glasses with his free hand. "At least, I didn't know until the day she hexed you. I could literally feel my connection to her when she was speaking that arcane curse, so I'm pretty sure I win the unfortunate family connection contest."

Orwin shuddered in revulsion.

"I wasn't aware there was such a contest," I quipped wryly, pulling the thick blanket a little tighter around my shoulders. We were somewhere in the middle of South Dakota at some random full-service campsite, and the temperature had to be in the mid-to-low thirties. Once the piercing wind picked up, we'd have no choice but to seek the warmth of the RV. Until then, I'd enjoy the crisp, fresh air instead of candy cane land. Not that I minded. I actually liked candy canes. "Ammeline probably doesn't even know she has any family left. She definitely didn't have all her faculties glued together the last time we saw her."

I believe you left off a fifth great in your long list of greats, if I've done my math correctly, Mr. Cornelia. As for the Lich's mental wellbeing, a witch is not meant to be on this earth past her natural mortality. No one is, in reality. There is no telling what danger our kind faces with such an abhorrent creature hiding in some cave while dancing around a cauldron in the nude. It's distasteful to even imagine the sight.

I lifted my face to the scattered flurries that were coming down from the overcast sky quite randomly, almost as if the clouds above weren't quite sure they should add more to the ground than what already blanketed the campsite. I understood its indecision, because I was faced with my own uncertainty over our immediate future.

Christmas was a week away, and this traveling family of mine deserved a timeout from this nonstop mystery solving cavalcade we'd found ourselves on this past year. Unfortunately, my hex might be a roadblock in their holiday vacation.

You're not the only one who is bothered by it, dear hexed one.

My traveling family consisted of myself, Orwin Cornelia, Piper and Pearl Allifair, and Knox Emeric. We each brought our own gifts to the table, though some in particular not by our own choice.

Orwin's reason for helping me with the search for a cure to my unfortunate hex had eventually become a need to right the wrong of his family bloodline. He was only twenty-one years old, though he was what I would definitely call an old soul. The elders of his family had known about Ammeline all along. Instead of warning the supernatural society that they were members of, they'd looked out for their own best interests, assuming no liability for their ancestor. Orwin wasn't exactly going to be welcomed back with open arms after his defiance of the elders' decisions concerning their family ties to Ammeline.

Piper was our Wiccan healer who understood the ramifications of letting someone like Ammeline Letty Romilda prey on other supernatural beings. At twenty-two, it was rather hard to believe that she was so kind, optimistic, and selfless at heart. She hadn't fallen prey to the naysayers, and I doubt she ever would, though it came across as her being a bit naïve.

Pearl, of course, wasn't about to let her charge go out into the world all by herself and unaware. The white short-haired domestic cat was one of royalty, dating all the way back to Queen Cleopatra's era. Long after the fall of the Egyptian Empire, Pearl had been discovered by an aristocratic archeologist who'd taken her back to England during the late 1800s. The wealth of knowledge that Pearl possessed was invaluable, and her mission was to guide Piper through her life…which was why she had come to accept Piper's rather considerable decision to rid the world of Ammeline's existence. No witch was meant to be immortal. It was a violation of the laws of the universe and a perversion of our faith and supernatural lifestyle. It had desiccated Ammeline's body and destroyed her mind until there was nothing left but a barren husk devoid of a soul.

That brought us to Knox Emeric, the mortal man who'd once been a war veteran searching for answers in the serenity of the forest when he discovered he was in the wrong place at the wrong time. I guess you could say he was much like me, only he'd come away from his run-in with Ammeline as a very special strain of lycanthrope. He was a former military special operator, protective by nature, and was all for justice served. Not a good combination to choose in a person when one decided to curse another with lycanthropy, born again as the vengeful werewolf of abnormal size and strength. Conquering the beast inside himself was a constant and difficult struggle.

Mr. Emeric is not just any werewolf, Miss Lilura. Being a Canis Lupus Occidentalis of the McKenzie Valley variant is rather prestigious. His species is royalty of its own kind. We all should be constantly mindful of that distinction. Speaking of our resident shapeshifter, shouldn't he have been back from his run by now? He said he was only ranging twenty miles.

I looked up at the overcast sky, though I could barely distinguish the outline of the full moon through the darkness. Knox had the special ability to transform at will, but the pull of a full moon was unusually strong. It was often too tough for him to resist the need to change. He didn't fight his curse, but instead allowed his inner beast to run free once a month. I admired the way he'd handled his transformation from a mere man into something that legends were made of in human folklore.

I took a sip of my hot chocolate, enjoying what was left of our evening. We didn't have many like this, and morning would come soon enough...along with the probability of having to solve another mystery. Our search for Ammeline was very limited to the little time we had in between us trying to prevent someone's death from happening or being forced to bring their killer to justice after the fact. You see, the hex that had ruined my life came in the form of horrific visions.

That's right—I had been cursed with premonitions of murder.

I must say, that last premonition was quite the doozy, dear hexed one. That poor man had been simply kissing his beloved wife underneath the mistletoe. Before we knew it, he'd all but collapsed into a heap onto the floor right next to that enormous Christmas tree. It was only due to the alien hunter's expertise in the strangest mix of specialties that we were able to find the location.

The alien hunter reference was due to the fact that Orwin was a bit of a conspiracy nut. I say that with complete affection, mind you, even though everyone was pretty sure he'd made all of us our own aluminum foil hats and stored them inside the RV somewhere as an emergency backup plan.

I no longer have to wonder how Mr. Cornelia came to be that way. Discovering oneself to be a distant blood relative of the infamous Lich Queen would have me seeing conspiracies around every corner, as well. I'll attempt to tone down my good-natured jesting, though I don't promise I'll always be able to keep my thoughts to myself.

"Like any time in the near future?" Orwin asked as he shot Pearl a sardonic glance.

She was currently sitting in the chair that Piper had occupied most of the evening before seeking privacy inside the RV to call her parents. At the age of twenty-two, I wasn't sure how she was going to explain that she couldn't make it home for the holidays. Another rush of fresh guilt hit my system.

"Truthfully, it wasn't that hard to locate the couple," Orwin replied with a shrug of modesty. "You were able to describe most of the ornaments on the tree, and the fact that there were two bulbs with the birthdates of their children was a goldmine of information, really. Then there was the genus of the tree and its distinct color of blue-green. It was a windfall."

I know I asked you this the other day, but have you seen a black van following us in the rearview mirror by chance?

"I'm offended you think I can't outsmart the infantile efforts of the NSA, cotton ball." Orwin pulled the cast iron pan closer to quickly glance at the chestnuts. "I'll have you know…"

While Orwin and Pearl debated over his ability versus the NSA's security measures, I enjoyed my hot chocolate and thought back to the premonition I'd had about Mr. Edgar Booneville all but collapsing from what looked to be a natural, everyday heart attack. Only I never had visions that didn't amount to murder of one sort or another, which put us directly on the path toward North Dakota.

Usually, my premonitions had around twenty-four hours before they came to fruition. Unfortunately, we'd been in South Carolina in search for Ammeline when I'd been hit with the effects of my hex. We'd tried our hardest to make it to our destination, but accidents and detours had us finally accepting that we wouldn't be able to prevent Mr. Booneville's unfortunate and untimely death. That was the hardest aspect of my curse to accept, and the weight of guilt that rested on my shoulders was astronomical.

Anyway, we'd ended up stopping at this campsite to stretch our collective legs and get some rest for what was sure to be a tough mystery to solve. If Mr. Booneville hadn't keeled over from a simple heart attack or some other natural cause, we'd have to wait for the autopsy report to give us the cause of death. In the meantime, we'd be well-rested to begin investigating who would want to kill the man in the first place. Better yet, who could benefit from murdering a sixty-seven-year-old retiree?

"No one is getting any rest until we get a timer for those strings of Christmas lights that are hung from one end of the RV to the other," Orwin said with determination, having picked up on my thoughts after he'd finished roasting the chestnuts over the campfire. He began peeling off the shells he'd already finished roasting so that he could then simmer the cooked nuts in butter and cinnamon with a bit of rosemary and a touch of unrefined sugar. My mouth was already watering. "By the way, Mr. Booneville had a life policy of only a half million dollars. His wife was the recipient. That's not a whole lot considering their lifestyle."

Suspect number one. My sweet Piper already has Mrs. Norma Booneville typed into that murder solving app of hers. It came in quite handy with that haunted house case we worked on a couple of months ago, although it didn't take into account actual supernatural spirits. That does make it tougher on those haunted house cases.

"Hey," Piper exclaimed after having opened the door on the RV. She was dressed in her plum winter jacket, with a matching scarf and a knit hat that had one of those holes on top for a ponytail. Her blonde curls bounced as her boots hit the ground. "Orwin, did you know that the small town we're driving to tomorrow is less than an hour away from that renowned UFO sighting in 1975? Dad mentioned it on our call. We'll have to scope it out when we're through with the case. By the way, Dad is sending us cookies to be delivered at the post office in Covered Bridge, North Dakota. I already went online and reserved a post office box in my name. We should be able to catch up on the mail."

Piper closed the distance to her chair where Pearl had been curled up and enjoying the heat. I didn't know if Piper's optimistic personality was due to her being a healer, but she definitely was the lone ray of sunshine in the group. Nothing ever brought her down, and she was always looking for that silver lining Pearl was trying to convince me existed.

You're not going into one of those moods of yours again, are you? Do you need to hear a knock-knock joke, dear hexed one?

"No, it's rather hard to have a pity party with 'Frosty the Snowman' playing in the background," I replied with a half-smile, focusing on Piper as she scooped Pearl up into her arms and took a seat. We all didn't need to be out in the middle of the wilderness this time of year, though. "Piper, I want you to know that you could always take the Jeep Wrangler and drive home for Christmas. Orwin and I can investigate this murder mystery, and then we'll meet up with you someplace between North Dakota and Pennsylvania."

"Is that what you're going to tell Knox?" Piper asked, her expressive blue eyes meeting mine over the fire. Determination and grit pretty much summed up the description of her tilted chin. "I'm believe I can answer for the both of us. We aren't going anywhere until Ammeline's cane is destroyed, the supernatural realm is safe, and the curses placed on you and Knox are lifted. See? Simple. Now, those chestnuts smell wonderful! You know, I've listened to that particular song so many times over the years, but I never imagined actually roasting chestnuts over an open fire. This is fun!"

By this time, Orwin had peeled off the shells from the first batch and was already in the process of allowing the nuts to swim in the simmering homemade coating he'd conjured up. It wouldn't be much longer before he served up the first batch of the delectable treat, piping hot from the pan.

My sweet Piper is getting very good at changing the subject, isn't she?

"Hush now," Piper scolded Pearl playfully. She adjusted Pearl on her lap as she settled more comfortably in the chair. "You know that I love the holidays. And there's no changing subjects when there's nothing left to talk about in regard to splitting up the group."

I'd already sensed a presence in the woods, so I wasn't startled when Knox materialized from the shadows. His short-cropped black hair was covered with a dark grey hat, and he was wearing a light winter jacket despite the near-freezing temperature, sans gloves. Steam seemed to rise off his person, though. Being a werewolf kept his body heat at a higher level than ours, as well as gave a shimmering appearance to those golden-brown eyes of his. He'd taken the time to dress after his shift from wolf, always mindful of Pearl's sense of etiquette, though I do believe he'd been raised to have a decent sense of modesty to begin with.

As it should be for every child who is raised to such standards as society dictates, Miss Lilura.

"What's this nonsense talk of splitting up?" Knox

asked without missing a step. His accusing gaze landed on me directly, knowing full well that I was the source of such a discussion. The thing of it was, he didn't have the family baggage that Orwin and I had in our lives. Knox's parents were human, fully believing their son needed some time to himself after multiple deployments in various warzones overseas. It wasn't fair that he was lying to them, and I bet going home for the holidays would mean the world to them. "It better be in regard to splitting up the rations of those chestnuts. I could smell them miles away on my run."

I daresay that the rich scent of those chestnuts covered up the wet dog odor quite nicely.

Knox had no idea that Pearl spoke disparagingly of his scent, because only witches, warlocks, and druids could hear the thoughts of familiars. Piper hid her smile behind one of her plum colored mittens.

"Almost done," Orwin said, giving the second set of chestnuts a bit more time to soak up the scrumptious flavor of the coating. "Hopefully, these are as good as you remember from your childhood, Lou. I had to look up the preparation process on the web."

I believe I'd like to try one with a spot of warm cream, Mr. Cornelia.

"I'll get you some," Piper offered, motioning for Orwin to stay by the fire so that the chestnuts could simmer in the rich sauce. "Be right back."

Thank you, dear. Oh, this will be such a treat indeed!

Orwin's nose was a bit red, but for once it wasn't due

to his allergic reaction to cats. That's right. He was allergic to Pearl, but the protection spell he'd warded himself with against any future run-ins with Ammeline was rather complicated to lower in order for Piper to heal him of such incidental reactions to common allergies.

It is one pesky complex spell, is it not?

"Knox, I'm just saying that your parents are worried about you, especially during this time of year," I said, attempting to ease into this conversation without Piper or Knox refuting my advice to spend time with their family. "And not just them, but also your extended family and friends. You're important to them, and vice versa. You are in complete control of your curse, and no one is going to be the wiser that you're actually anything other than what you appear to be."

Knox leaned back in his chair after he'd taken a bottle of water out of his cup holder. Changing always seemed to make him thirsty. I don't believe I'd ever seen him drink anything other than water or coffee. He tilted the bottle, though he didn't remove his focus from me. It was as if he was attempting to figure out why I was so determined to get him to visit home for the holidays.

It didn't take a genius to figure out that I had family issues of my own, and I didn't want to see him go down the same road. I honestly didn't regret leaving my coven at the age of seventeen. Believe it or not, a lot of witches and wizards chose to try and live a normal life outside of witchcraft's traditional tightknit community and cloistered way of life. Unfortunately, my parents had been the head of the council of the infamous Salem coven. They believed my choice to be an insult to their leadership. Needless to say, our parting wasn't the sappy stuff from the movies, but rather akin to a shunning.

Have you considered that maybe it's time to let bygones be bygones? You won't know if they feel the same unless we pay them a visit, dear hexed one.

I wasn't even remotely considering that option at the moment, especially because I'd have to confess that I'd been hexed by the notorious Ammeline Letty Romilda for all my efforts. If I thought they'd been disappointed by my decision to leave the coven, I could only imagine how disgraced they would feel to find out they actually had a daughter hexed by the Lich Queen.

Maybe that was why it was so much easier to focus on Knox and Piper's families than my own. Piper's family was proud of her decision, whereas Knox had just chosen to leave his family and friends behind, worried about his wellbeing and his whereabouts.

"I'll return home when our curses are lifted and Ammeline is in the afterlife where she belongs," Knox reiterated for what had to be the hundredth time. If anyone could hear us, they'd probably believe we were horrible people bent on revenge. The truth of the matter was that Ammeline had died hundreds of years ago, and the only thing left was her essence that she'd magically confined into a phylactery through the use of a series of arcane black necromancy and transmutation spells. "So, have we learned anything more on the Booneville case?"

I guess that answers your question, dear hexed one. Oh, look! My sweet Piper has returned with my spot of warm cream. It's all about the simple pleasures in life, really. You should shorten your expectations once in a while.

"Only that Norma Booneville inherited five hundred thousand dollars when good ol' Edgar kicked the bucket," Orwin shared, finally deciding that the chestnuts were finished and ready to be enjoyed. He began dishing them out in plastic bowls. "Once we go back inside the RV, I'll spend the rest of the evening putting together a dossier on the Boonevilles' finances. We'll be set to drive into Covered Bridge, North Dakota tomorrow morning."

Piper had brought out a small stool that Pearl could sit on while she drank her spot of warm cream and enjoyed her first taste of roasted chestnuts. The small pedestal kept her up out of the snow, while maintaining a close distance to the warmth of the fire.

Piper began talking about the UFO sighting in 1975, which started a long-winded explanation from Orwin about what actually occurred during that incident. We might tease him about his obsession with conspiracy theories that ranged from UFOs to JFK, but he was a wealth of knowledge about these subjects, which made for interesting conversations around the campfire.

Our days were usually so busy with hunting Ammeline, preventing murders, or solving murder mysteries that we rarely got time to enjoy times like these as a group. Orwin spent a lot of time on the computer using his technological abilities to aid our investigations. Knox didn't ride along with us, but instead followed behind in his Land Rover, occasionally crashing on the couch in the RV. Quite often he even detoured on side missions in our search for Ammeline, looking for anyone or anything that could help in the hunt. After all, he was a hunter by nature.

That left Piper and I, who were usually so tired that one of us went to bed early, leaving one of us or the other to hang with Pearl in the evening. It was rare that we were all around the campfire like this evening, enjoying each other's company.

Knox's rich laughter filled the air when Piper relayed a quip from Pearl regarding little green men. Orwin accepted the jesting good-naturedly, having sat back in his chair to enjoy his creation. I savored everyone's enjoyment in this moment while relishing the delicious chestnut treats that I hadn't enjoyed since being a teenager back home.

It's nice to see you appreciating life's little moments, dear hexed one. One never knows what tomorrow may bring. Well, we technically do know what is on our agenda—a murder mystery that begins with a kiss under the mistletoe!

Chapter Two

"THIS IS EXACTLY why you shouldn't kiss someone underneath the mistletoe," I muttered from the driver's seat of my red Jeep Wrangler. She was my 4x4 baby, and I'd had her since my seventeenth birthday. I didn't even look at the mileage anymore, because it didn't matter for anything other than oil changes. She'd stay with me until her engine fell out of the bottom. I just had to make sure I never shared a kiss underneath a sprig of mistletoe. "How is this even possible?"

I can see that this is your way of talking yourself out of an intimate moment with our resident wolfman, but I'm pretty sure that my pristine white fur still has few singes on it from those searing looks that passed between the two of you last night.

"Have you and Piper been streaming the Hallmark Channel again on her laptop?" I wasn't going to waste the day talking about some imaginary chemistry that Pearl believed existed between me and Knox. We had one vile Lich and two curses that connected us, from which a friendship had developed. Nothing more, nothing less. "And I take back my inquiry of how good ol' Edgar could keel over from ingesting too much Christmas spirit. It wasn't the kiss. Someone clearly poisoned him, and now it's been determined to be an official homicide case."

Piper and I were going over every lead detailed in the police report on the pending case that Orwin had hacked into for us before leaving the campsite this morning. We'd gotten up early and driven the rest of the mileage to another full-service campsite right outside of a small town called Covered Bridge. Campsites this far north were fewer and farther between now that their summer tourist season was over; however, those that were near large ski resorts with a multitude of snowmobile trails were still open for campers. Many of them even had heated shower facilities for the RV crowd and limited two hundred and twenty volt drops for the luxury models.

"Speaking of Hallmark movies, this town could literally be the set for one," Piper exclaimed in disbelief, leaning forward to get a better look at the twenty-six foot Christmas tree that was smack-dab in the middle of the town square and decorated to the hilt. The residents were already milling about with their steaming cups of hot coffee, all bundled up to keep Jack Frost at bay. Most of the townsfolk smiled and waved at one another, with a few of them even stopping to chat about what was sure to be today's gossip—that one of their very own had been murdered. "Look at the awnings of those shops. And the lampposts are straight out of a Norman Rockwell painting. I thought my hometown was charming, but we have nothing on this place. Have you ever seen anything so quaint outside of a scene on a Christmas card?"

"If you spy a coffee shop, I'll call anything you want quaint." I flipped the page while scanning Norma Booneville's information. "Who would have thought that knitting was so lucrative? I mean, the Boonevilles have an entire shop devoted to the hobby."

History books claim that the origins for knitting came from the Middle East. Little do they know that it actually originated from the Egyptian Empire. Who knew that my beloved Cleopatra had been a trendsetter? She was always a bit of a free spirit.

"I've been wanting to get back into knitting," Piper shared, peering past me to see what shops were lined up on the left side of the street. She was wearing her plum winter jacket again, with the knitted mittens, scarf, and hat that had the small hole in the top for her ponytail. She patted said hat and adjusted her hair. "Just think, I could make us one in every color. Hey, there's the café. Should we grab you a coffee and me a tea before heading over to the knitting shop? It's doubtful that Mrs. Booneville will be there, but we'll probably get to talk with one of her employees. Maybe we can listen in on the local gossip devotees who happen to be hanging out hoping for some juicy tidbits. Then we really should seek out any members of Mr. and Mrs. Booneville's bridge club."

I'd stopped listening to our extensive to-do list after Piper had mentioned coffee. It was my version of sanity in a cup. If there was any more talk of knitting hats in every color of the rainbow, I was definitely going to need more than what I'd drank on the short drive here from the campsite.

I wasn't the kind of woman who wore knitted hats and gloves, but not for the reasons you might think. I'm pretty sure it was due to the fact that I'd been cursed by the Lich Queen during broad daylight in public. Hats and mittens caused me to feel confined, though I did manage to wear insulated leather gloves when the weather became too cold. By too cold, I mean below freezing temperatures.

A quick glance in the rearview mirror reflected my porcelain skin and high cheekbones. I didn't have curls the way Piper did, so I doubt my long black hair would have looked the same in that plum hat of hers.

My sweet Piper once tried to knit me a sweater, bless her heart.

Pearl might be a wealth of old English sayings, but she did try to insert one or two American maxims in the mix when it was appropriate. She also had quite the taste for the occasional connotation, because I could just imagine her appalled expression upon seeing a cat sweater knitted in a deep purple hue. I didn't bother to hide my smile, which was what Pearl always seemed to be vying for these days.

I thought you might find the image of me in a plum knit sweater humorous, dear hexed one.

"How long did it take for you to unravel the sweater?" I inquired, knowing full well Piper was listening in on our conversation. She'd rolled her blue eyes twice at Pearl's commentary. "Oh, I so would have paid to see that."

"You two have your fun. Just know that you two will be matching come Christmas morning," Piper warned, reaching for the handle on her door. "Let's grab our tea and coffee ration. We'll take them with us over to the knitting store."

"I blame you for this," I muttered, shutting off the engine after Piper had closed her door. "We'll all be walking around looking like knitted little gnomes in neon pink."

I slid the stack of papers I still held in my hand in between my seat and the middle console. It wouldn't do to have someone walking past the Jeep and spying the initial medical findings for Edgar Booneville's autopsy laying out in plain sight. Too many questions weren't a good thing when we were trying to fly under the radar.

My sweet Piper has a mind of her own, Miss Lilura. Knitting is a healthy outlet…as long as I'm not the recipient of said gift.

"In case you missed it, your sweet Piper included you in that matching hat threat of hers." I palmed my keys before opening my door. "You should have taught her to do crossword puzzles."

"At least we don't stand out like they do," Piper whispered after I'd joined her to walk across the street. I made sure to press the key fob so that my baby was locked up tight. "Oh, look. There's Orwin."

The town of Covered Bridge, North Dakota didn't have a police force. Therefore, the murder of Edgar Booneville had fallen to the state police. The detectives were easily distinguishable due to their suits and close-cropped military style haircuts. We'd come to find in previous investigations that the police didn't include everything in their reports. Orwin had quickly ascertained which detectives had been assigned to the murder case, and he would get within range of the duo to see what was being left out of the report that may help us figure out who poisoned good ol' Edgar.

Being in a large group attracted too much attention, anyway. With Orwin blending in with the residents, the detectives shouldn't become too suspicious at seeing him around town. Knox, on the other hand, had gone straight for the Booneville residence. He'd wanted to see who was coming and going, as well as to see if Mrs. Booneville drove anywhere suspicious. His ability to track any subject was unparalleled. Of course, that was a symptom of his curse—tracking prey was basically imprinted on his primary senses now. In werewolf form, any human adversary would be at a distinct disadvantage…even an armed one.

It appears we have all the angles covered, dear hexed one.

"With any luck, we'll figure out this murder mystery in the next day or two." I didn't miss Piper's quick glance as we finally stepped onto the curb right in front of the coffee shop. It wasn't the heat of her stare that had me shaking my head, but instead the weight of Pearl's brooding gaze. She'd made sure she was invisible, but that didn't mean I couldn't sense when she was judging me. "What? It's Christmastime. I can be a little optimistic, can't I? Maybe we can rent one of the cottages over at the campground and enjoy Christmas morning in front of a roaring fireplace with a real Christmas tree."

I do believe the thought of you being overly optimistic would actually occur when Hades froze over, but by all means…continue to astound us, dear hexed one.

Piper didn't bother to contain her laugh as she reached for the door handle, but she stopped just in time before two older ladies stepped outside first.

"…heard it was murder," a silver haired woman exclaimed in horror. She was carrying a cup holder with all four slots filled with drinks. She gave us an apologetic smile before returning to her conversation. "I bet it's that no-good son-in-law of theirs. Did you see the car that he and Abigail drove into town? Just disgraceful!"

"Do you remember that horrible fight Norma and Abigail had right before the wedding?" the other woman inquired, never once looking our way as she tossed her question over her shoulder. She had a reddish tint to her stylish hairdo, and it was evident that she had the roots touched up frequently. "Norma warned that girl that Patrick was bad news, even back then. I heard that…"

My sweet Piper already added in the daughter and son-in-law to that app of hers. Mr. Cornelia did a bit of digging into those two, and it appears that the two of them had been over for dinner the night of Mr. Booneville's demise.

"She was carrying a tray of coffees," Piper pointed out, keeping her voice hushed as we made our way directly to the counter. The layout of this café made it relatively easy to place an order, basically ushering those who waited for their coffee toward the side counter so that the patrons weren't blocking the entrance. "The other woman had a box of pastries. Maybe they're heading over to the Booneville residence or maybe the knitting circle."

"Well, if they're talking about the suspected poisoning, so is everyone else," I presumed, hoping we'd catch some of the gossip flying around about the murder. "Keep your ear low to the ground."

There was one woman ahead of us with a group of teenagers. They were only concerned with Christmas shopping, talking amongst each other about what sales were going on in town. There was even mention of driving to the nearest mall, but that was at least a twenty-three-mile drive down the interstate to the next larger town. A part of me felt a bit bad for the mother who would be chauffeuring four teenage girls to the mall all hopped up on caffeine. Maybe they should opt out and go for the hot chocolate instead.

I completely relate, as I have two of my own to keep up with. I'm not so sure I would have the patience to oversee two more. I'll go make my rounds now, dear hexed one.

Piper nudged me a bit, tilting her head ever so slightly to newspaper rack positioned to our right. It had one national newspaper on the second tier, while the local *Covered Bridge Gazette* held stature on the top. Sure enough, Edgar Booneville's picture had made the front page on this morning's edition.

"Piper, look at that," I said in a normal tone so that anyone in our vicinity could hear me. It was likely that we'd already drawn a few curious glances since we weren't from here, but the fact that it was Christmastime would be to our benefit. We'd already come up with a cover story about being from the next town over, wanting to hit some of the local shops for the last-minute sales. "Grandma Tilly was talking about that poor man this morning. He was the lawyer who drew up her will. She couldn't believe that someone would want to murder such a sweet man."

"Mr. Booneville was so nice," one of the girls gushed as she made no effort to hide the fact that she'd heard me. Her pink lipstick matched the scarf she was wearing, as did her cheeks. "We were all talking about him on the drive over here. What happened to him must have been an accidental poisoning or something like that."

"Yeah, like, we were thinking maybe he drank something by mistake," one of the other girls said, stepping forward when it was their turn in line. She turned back toward us to add one more crucial bit of information. "Mrs. Booneville was always complaining about how her husband never looked up from those contracts he always had in front of him."

"Girls." The mother gave Piper and I both a cautious stare, having realized that we were complete strangers. "Give Marcie your order."

Well, that was the end of that scavenger hunt.

"Don't mind her," a woman said behind us, drawing our attention away from the young girls in front of us. "That's Jill. She doesn't trust anyone—not even her own husband. And for good reason with that one."

Oh, my gracious! I'm gone for one minute, and the two of you have somehow gone and attracted a charlatan. I do hope that Mr. Cornelia is having better luck than we are.

"Hi," Piper exclaimed, holding out her hand in greeting. "I'm Piper. This is Lou. We're here doing a little Christmas shopping, but we just read what happened to that poor man."

"Don't feel too bad, dear. Edgar had the people of this town snowed under year-round…no pun intended. I'm Gracie Lynn Hauver," the woman replied with a smile. Her bracelets all clinked together when she returned Piper's handshake. "You'll want to stop by Go

Out In Style, the boutique two blocks down. They'll be having a thirty percent off flash sale in about twenty minutes."

By this time, all the young teens had placed their orders and were now whispering amongst each other that they needed to quickly get to the boutique before anyone else got what they were looking for on sale. The mother, Jill, shot Gracie a rather skeptical glance. It appeared that no one quite knew whether or not to believe if Grace was a bona fide fortune teller.

If she pulls out a business card, I'm going to guess the latter, dear hexed one.

"If you'd like to know where the other sales are, feel free to stop by my parlor next to the Four-Leaf Clover." Gracie had somehow produced said business card without ever reaching into her oversized purse. I'm pretty she'd had it hidden up the sleeve of her flowy emerald green blouse. "I accept donations for my sessions, of course."

I feel I should touch on a couple of things, Miss Lilura. The first is that flowy is just a description. Our local fortune teller wears belle sleeves. You might want to brush up on your fashion terminology. As for the donations part of this discussion, she's basically saying you have the word gullible *written across your forehead.*

"We may just do that," I replied with a smile of my own, taking Gracie's card and feigning interest in the fact that there was a crystal ball directly in the center of the rectangle. I purposefully let my grin fade and my expression turn into one of worry. "Although, I'm not so sure we should stay around town if someone who lives here is capable of murder. You can't be too careful."

Piper nudged my arm, causing me to look over my shoulder. The barista was waiting impatiently for us to step forward, and we'd also garnered most of the patrons' attention. No one hid the fact that they were now hanging onto our every word.

It's not you or my sweet Piper who has their attention, dear hexed one. The locals may be very vocal about their distrust of their resident fortune teller, but there is a part of them that is quite wary she might actually have the gift. They are eager to hear what she has to say about the murder.

"I've already given my statement to the detectives in charge of the case," Gracie revealed, waving her hand in the direction of another location. The dramatic flourish caused her bracelets to ring their melodic tune, giving her the theatrical flair she'd wanted all along. "The residents of this town are safe from harm. I know that beyond a shadow of a doubt."

Once again, where is the alien hunter when needed? Our local fortune teller is no witch, nor does she have any gift, as far as I can tell. Therefore, I am not privy to her thoughts. With that said, I do believe that I've gotten a hint of wet dog underneath a fairly heavy dose of perfume. Corner table.

"We'll have one coffee with a double shot of…"

Piper placed our order as I zeroed in on the long-haired brunette who was texting on her phone while seemingly waiting for someone to join her, if the second cup of coffee was anything to go by. She was stunningly beautiful with a flawless complexion and full lips that usually came from repeated injections of Botox. In her case, I'm pretty sure it was natural.

What was a werewolf doing in a small town like Covered Bridge?

I presume Christmas shopping. Most supernatural beings do partake in the holidays. One shouldn't judge a book by its cover, Miss Lilura.

Piper finished placing our order, so I took out a five and a couple of ones from my coat pocket, leaving the barista a decent tip. We took our place behind the teenagers near the pick-up counter. I made sure to stand at an angle so that I could keep an eye on the she-wolf.

She-wolf? Well, that's certainly an appropriate nickname, though I seem to detect a bit of wariness in your tone. I didn't realize that you were so suspicious of other supernatural beings, dear hexed one.

I wasn't in the least distrustful of other supernatural beings. Well, if I discounted Ammeline Letty Romilda, of course. I should definitely have phrased my curiosity in a different way, such as why this particular she-wolf was not with her pack at the moment. Pearl would have picked up the scent the moment we crossed into town had this been a sanctuary for an actual den of were-wolves.

I guess when you put it that way, a bit of wariness is warranted. Our she-wolf seems to be done waiting for her guest. She's collecting her belongings, Miss Lilura. Would you like me to follow her?

This case had taken a turn that we hadn't expected, somehow including a bogus fortune teller and a she-wolf in the blink of an eye. I'd held out hope this was an easy mystery to solve. It appeared I wasn't going to get my Christmas wish this year, so I reluctantly agreed that the best course of action was to allow Pearl to follow one of these leads.

Your Christmas wish could still come true, dear hexed one. Never lose hope. Now, off I go to see if I can scrounge up a Christmas miracle for us all!

Chapter Three

"CAN YOU SEND a text to Orwin?" I requested, sipping my hot beverage to help stave off the winter chill. We'd collected our drinks and exited the tea shop, waiting to talk freely after the door had closed behind us. The first thing Piper had done was pull out her phone to input the supposed seer's name and description of the unknown girl into her app. "Ask him to try and find out what Gracie Lynn told those detectives. She made it sound as if she actually had some kind of information on who might have murdered Edgar."

I'd already looked around the area discreetly, but I didn't notice anything amiss. With that said, there was something about having another werewolf around this case that made me feel itchy, and it wasn't because of a bad case of the fleas.

Was that a joke, dear hexed one? It did make me smile for a moment.

"What are you doing back so soon?" Piper asked, having already slipped her phone back inside her pocket.

How she hadn't spilled her tea was beyond me. "Where did she go?"

Our little she-wolf walked over to the diner, where she joined a friend. Are we heading for the knitting shop?

Piper and I exchanged glances of skepticism at the way Pearl had answered and immediately changed topics. There hadn't been enough time to make any kind of assessment regarding the she-wolf. I could only imagine the reaction we were going to get once Little Miss Wolfy got a sniffer full of our guy. The fur would surely hit the fan then.

Oh, look, my sweet Piper! It's an elf handing out chocolate. Isn't that just charming?

Sure enough, a tiny woman around five feet tall had dressed up as an elf and was standing outside a chocolate and fudge shop called Chocoholics Reunion. It was a cute name, and the chocolates were even more adorable in the shape of candy canes. Piper immediately took one with a promise to return, explaining we were on our way to the knitting shop. I did my best to ignore the temptation, but the delightful elf had a way about her that made it hard to say no. Chocolate and coffee together should fall under one of the seven deadly sins, but I would gladly take a trip to Hades in a one horse open sleigh if I could eat one of these delicious morsels every single day.

Here we are! Oh, look at that colorful yarn. I've got a hankering to unwind that ball of mesmerizing sparkles for some odd reason.

I swallowed the last bit of melted chocolate on my tongue, realizing that Piper and I had been duped by a very cunning familiar. She'd used our love of delectable treats to avoid answering why the she-wolf wasn't important to our case any longer. The topic would have to be shelved for five minutes while Piper and I paid a visit to one of Norma Booneville's employees.

"Good morning," an older woman called out with a smile from behind the counter. "Please take a look around. Don't hesitate to ask if you have any questions."

"Thank you," Piper called out, leaving my side and immediately making her way over to a bin of yarn that consisted of every Christmas color splashed on a tree. "This is perfect!"

There were two customers waiting in line to check out, as well as two others browsing the inventory of yarn. Piper was *oohing* and *ahhing* over the inventory, causing me to wish I'd taken the task of staking out the Booneville residence myself. I couldn't help but smile at the picture of Knox standing in a shop like this, frozen with fear and surrounded by admiring old ladies.

These colors are just darling, aren't they?

Pearl had just tipped her hand, because there was no way she was going to allow Piper to stock up on yarn. We'd end up looking like twins in a knitting nightmare featuring matching hats, mittens, and scarves.

I have no idea what you're referring to, dear hexed one. Do you see that silver ball of yarn? I was hoping to get Piper to make a knitted hat with little foil antennas for the alien hunter as a gift from me. I think it would be a rather clever gift, if I do say so myself.

"…just awful," one of the women said in a hushed voice. "I heard that Esther and Sandra went over to Norma's house with some pastries. I think those two busybodies just went over there to see what the detectives had to say about the autopsy report."

The other woman concurred, but it was Piper who now had my attention when she handed me her phone. I held my coffee cup in my left hand while I took the cell phone from her, reading Orwin's reply about the local fortune teller.

By the look on your face, dear hexed one, it appears as if Mr. Cornelia might have just granted you a Christmas wish.

"Piper, I'll be right back," I said, nodding to the ladies who were still discussing Edgar Booneville's death. I made sure to hand Piper her phone back. "I like the black yarn with the silver thread. Pearl likes the red and blue one."

Heaven to Betsy! I uttered not one word about…

One point to me in whatever game it was that Pearl was playing by not sharing information about the she-wolf. It wasn't like I wouldn't figure out what was going on sooner rather than later, but right now I needed to speak with Orwin. His text indicated that he'd veered away from the detectives to chase down a lead on our local fortune teller.

I scanned the shops that were lined up across the

street, looking for one called the Four-Leaf Clover. Sure enough, the hand-painted green little weed wasn't hard to miss on the display window. I finally spotted Orwin and quickly made my way across the street toward him.

"Hey," I called out, my lungs aching as I breathed in too much of the cold morning air. "What did you find out?"

"I found out that this town has the best blueberry scones I've ever tasted," Orwin replied, holding up an empty napkin. There wasn't the slightest crumb left. "Whoever makes them over at the bakery could win one of those television shows that Piper always streams on her laptop."

I would have mentioned the chocolate candy canes, but I was afraid we'd never get to the heart of the matter at hand. Even now, my taste buds were salivating for more.

"Right," Orwin said after I'd given him a pointed look. "I'm going to go see a fortune teller. Apparently, Detectives Hadden and Fisher believe that she might have something to do with Edgar Booneville's death. Long story short, her lease is up at the end of the year."

"You mean, end of the year as in two weeks from now?"

"Yep," Orwin replied with an affirmative nod. "Gracie Lynn believes that her contract offered her the option of staying for an additional year, but the landlord said he can override that addendum—which he did in the time stipulated. The fortune teller apparently reached out to good ol' Edgar to look over the contract, but he agreed that the landlord would win should she take it to court. Let's just say that she wasn't happy, and there might have been a very public scene at the diner between them not too long ago. Oh, and get this…the landlord told the detectives that he thinks Gracie Lynn put a curse on Edgar. Can you imagine?"

"A curse? Like she would even be able to do such a thing."

Where have I heard that one before? In all seriousness, though, I guess it made sense. Anytime someone was a bit different from what they believed was the norm, people became wary. Rumors would get started, gossip would circle, and then a person's life could burst into flames…all because they were a little odd.

Unfortunately, Gracie Lynn Hauver wasn't helping those innocent people out by pretending to be something she wasn't just to make twenty dollars by providing bogus readings. I did a double take at the sign in the window. Twenty dollars?

"You read it right." Orwin shook his head at the expensive payment, although the smaller print did say that it was simply a donation and that the so-called *reading* was entirely for entertainment purposes. "I'm trying really hard not to be insulted here."

I completely understood Orwin's stance on the subject, because Gracie Lynn was basically making a mockery of our way of life. We needed to look past that, though, and determine if she was actually capable of murder.

"Anyone is capable of murder," Orwin simply stated, as if he truly believed that sentiment. He shrugged before tossing the balled-up napkin into a barreled trashcan. "Why are you staring at me like that? It's completely true."

"Because I think that Pearl set her sights on the wrong target," I muttered, shaking my head at Orwin's cynicism. "And yes, I'm totally throwing you under the bus. I've had enough knock-knock jokes to last me a lifetime. Hey, after you're done paying your hard-earned twenty bucks to see if Gracie Lynn actually did murder Edgar, would you take a walk down to the diner? There's a she-wolf in town, and I'd like to know why. Pearl is pretty sure that the woman is alone, although she did meet up with a non-supernatural friend. I think. I honestly don't know, because Pearl is being tight-lipped about what she found out."

"She-wolf?"

I didn't bother to respond to Orwin about the nickname I'd given the werewolf, having been through that once already with Pearl. Besides, there was something more going on with the situation that Pearl was intentionally keeping from me. She'd never deliberately done something like that before…it was so underhanded.

"Underhanded?" Orwin asked in surprise, utterly

fascinated that our etiquette-obsessed feline had done something so rude. "You now have my full attention."

"Excuse me," a man said in a concise tone, stepping around us as he reached for the shop's door.

It just so happened to be one of the detectives who Orwin had been following around this morning. A quick look over my shoulder revealed that his partner was a few steps behind, slipping a cell phone into his heavy wool dress coat. Their expressions told me that something interesting was about to happen.

"They're going to be taking her in for official questioning," Orwin murmured after the door had closed behind the two detectives. He shook his head in frustration. "I didn't get more than that when they walked by, but I don't think I'm going to be able to get close for a long enough period of time to pick up on Gracie Lynn's thoughts. They'll know something is up if I'm still standing here when they come out."

"Are you sure the police are just questioning her and not making an arrest?" I asked, wrapping my right arm around my waist in an effort to remain warm. I held the coffee cup to my mouth, hoping the bit of steam coming out of the slit in the cover would give my lips a bit of heat. Going from shop to shop hadn't been too bad, but standing out in this cold weather was something else altogether. "We haven't had much luck in past cases when it came to police involvement, but it's possible the detectives can prove that she was the one who poisoned

Edgar Booneville."

"No," Orwin responded, shooting down any hopes that this murder mystery would be solved before lunchtime. "The fortune teller is basically their only suspect, besides the wife, of course. That's due to the life insurance policy. As for the daughter and son-in-law, they aren't even on the detectives' radars. Have you heard from Knox?"

"No, but he was just keeping an eye on the Booneville residence. I doubt anything exciting has happened over there except a lot of guests stopping in with food dishes." I glanced across the street to see the two women who'd been inside the knitting shop step out onto the sidewalk. Piper was still inside, which meant she might have snuck a moment of privacy to speak with Norma's employee. "I'm heading back over to the knitting shop. Keep me posted on what you find out here."

I carefully made my way back across the street, mindful of the small spots of ice and packed snow. Sure enough, I spotted Piper through the glass display window. She was deep in conversation with the employee behind the counter.

Welcome back, Miss Lilura. The woman's name is Julie Kirkham. She's not only an employee of the knitting shop, but she's also a very good friend of Mrs. Booneville. A wealth of information, I tell you. Now come in out of the cold, dear hexed one. Hurry now. No need to tempt Jack Frost. I hear he has a nasty bite.

Once again, I was astonished at Pearl's complete one-eighty. It was as if she'd been taken over by one of Orwin's pod people that he claimed was another competing alien race that had visited earth for thousands of years. I'd already had my bare hand on the door handle, getting ready to pull it open when an inherent need to look over my shoulder was just too tempting.

Miss Lilura, I think it best that—

I had to blink a couple of times to make sure that my eyes weren't deceiving me. It didn't take long for the coldness of the handle to seep into my hand, which I yanked back before I ended with that frostbite Pearl had so playfully mentioned. It was what she hadn't revealed that was the problem—Knox was the friend that the she-wolf was meeting with. He'd stepped outside the diner with his hand very casually placed in the middle of her lower back.

"You knew all along," I whispered harshly, grateful when no one was around to hear me. "Not nice, Pearl."

I'm sure that it's not what it looks like, just as I'm certain there is a reasonable explanation as to why our stalwart werewolf isn't at the Booneville residence. I didn't mention that the friend our she-wolf had met up with was none other than Mr. Emeric due to my concern that you'd have this very reaction.

I wasn't sure how else I was supposed to react to the fact that one of my team members had blatantly lied about being somewhere he wasn't. As a matter of fact, he was supposed to be helping with the case so that he could go home to visit his family for the holidays.

Technically, that was your wish for him, Miss Lilura. Mr. Emeric has made it quite clear that he doesn't intend to return back home until after he is rid of his lycanthropy curse. I'm sure that the she-wolf is nothing more than a mere acquaintance. There is no need for—

"So help me, Pearl, if you believe for one second that I'm jealous," I muttered in a dare, while watching the she-wolf laugh at something Knox had said.

I'd like to go on record that I'm not envious at all. I'm protective of my inner circle, that's all. I also might or might not agree with Orwin's statement earlier about anyone being capable of murder.

Oh, dear. I do believe it's time for one of my special holiday knock-knock jokes…

Chapter Four

"...SO BAD FOR her," Julie finished saying as she stepped around the counter. She dabbed a convenient tissue underneath her eye, making sure that she hadn't smeared her mascara. "Edgar had put off retirement until just this past week, mostly because he was a workaholic and just couldn't help himself. Norma had all sorts of things planned to keep him busy, but...well, I guess now it doesn't matter. Anyway, I'll make sure to tell her that your grandmother sends her condolences."

I'd opted to reenter the knitting shop, leaving the whole Knox situation to Orwin. I refused to even contemplate how Knox knew that woman outside of the obvious, because all it would do was give Pearl fodder to keep those knock-knock jokes coming until I was begging for a few of those little green men to come take me away. I did wonder if my curse would still work in outer space. I imagined it would work no matter how far I traveled away from here. Running from my problems seldom did anything but complicate my situation.

Let's not find out, shall we? Instead, I'll finish catching you up on Mrs. Kirkham. She not only works here part-time, but she and her husband are part of the bridge club that meets every Thursday evening. My sweet Piper couldn't get a word out of her until she made up a story that her grandmother knew Mrs. Booneville from a chance encounter during a knitting convention years ago.

There were knitting conventions? Who knew?

It was then that I witnessed the colossal amount of yarn in Piper's arms. I took another swallow of my coffee to keep from picturing myself in knitted accessories from head to toe. Piper had said that she wanted to up her game in the knitting department, but Pearl had mentioned a sweater project that had ended up going horribly awry. What were the chances that Piper could actually learn the proper way and work on such complicated patterns while travelling around the country in an RV?

I do believe that this quaint little store has created a knitting monster, and please don't put anything past my sweet Piper. She can be very determined when she sets her mind on something.

"I just saw two detectives enter the fortune teller's shop," I added into the conversation, twisting slightly with a pointed finger. "Do you think that she has something to do with Mr. Booneville's murder?"

"It's not surprising that the detectives sought Gracie Lynn out," Julie said a bit haughtily with a single sniff as she reached out to lighten Piper's burden. "Everyone knows about the argument she had with Edgar over at the diner. As a matter of fact, there's some speculation that she might have actually placed a curse on him. She can be spiteful."

"You don't believe that, do you?" Piper asked in a hushed tone, as if she wasn't sure curses were real or not. "I mean, a curse? Really? Witches aren't real, right?"

I find it quite strange that a woman who is supposed to be friends with the Boonevilles doesn't seem to be a bit more upset. I mean, a good friend of hers did just died.

Pearl had a point, but we'd learned a while back that not everyone grieved the same way in the midst of all of our cases.

"I'm not denying that some of Gracie Lynn's predictions come true, but I don't know about a curse. It sounds like complete nonsense to me," Julie said with a wave of her hand. "Norma spoke to those detectives first thing this morning, and apparently Edgar was poisoned."

"Who else had a problem with Edgar besides Gracie Lynn?" I asked, biting my lip when I realized that I'd asked that particular question too soon. Julie drew back a bit after she'd set Piper's items on the counter, regarding me warily. "It's just that Piper's grandmother thought the world of Norma. I can't imagine that being a small-town lawyer would attract those type of criminal elements, if you know what I mean. Could it simply have been an accidental poisoning, like with garden insecticides or something like that around the house?"

Nice recovery, dear hexed one. I'm sure there's a random person or two who haven't heard what type of poison was used on poor Mr. Booneville.

"You know, that's exactly what I said on the phone to Norma this morning." Julie walked over to the wall with hooks that contained every size needle a knitter could ask for, choosing a couple of packets and handing them off to Piper. "Don't get me wrong. I've seen Gracie Lynn angry before, and it's not pretty. But to poison someone? Well, things like that don't happen here in Covered Bridge. People just don't go around here doing that sort of thing."

Considering that a she-wolf walked amongst the residents of this quaint little town, I had a feeling that Julie nor the rest of the townsfolk didn't know of everything that went on in Covered Bridge.

Touché, Miss Lilura. I do believe I can still detect a bit of resentment at me for attempting to spare your feelings, though. We should work on that. It does not bode well to keep things bottled up inside over long periods of time. Maybe we should try some free association later…possibly try punching some balls of yarn to work off that stress.

I drained what was left of my coffee, already knowing that another one was in my near future. My phone vibrating was the perfect excuse I had for leaving Piper here to finish up her shopping while I made my way back to the café. I'd all but said as much as I turned on the heels of my well-worn Ugg boots that I'd bought last year before the start of the season. An informative text from Orwin had me stopping in my tracks.

"Um, Mrs. Kirkham?" I turned around to find Julie

showing Piper several books with numerous patterns that she could choose from. The older woman pasted a smile on her face as she raised a brow in question. "Do you know Mr. and Mrs. Wilkes?"

"Why, yes," Julie replied, straightening her shoulders a bit as she gathered her wits. "Roger and Debbie were good friends of ours. Why do you ask?"

It was evident from the way that Julie reversed direction and took the pattern books over to the cash register that she was ready to ring up Piper's items and send us on our way. Julie's nervous response told me that Orwin was onto something, and my morning was finally picking up.

Piper, my sweet darling, you're going to want to enter those two names into your app under the suspect column. We could be closer to solving our mystery. Oh, and Miss Lilura? I would tread carefully with this line of questioning. Mrs. Kirkham seems a bit shaken that you would mention the Wilkes.

"Oh, we were just hoping they still resided in Covered Bridge," I replied with a small shrug, taking Pearl's advice. Even I could see the slight tremor in Julie's right hand. "Piper's grandmother wanted us to say hello to Mrs. Wilkes."

"I do believe they still live over on Passage Lane," Julie commented vaguely, beginning to ring up Piper's order. She was rather swift at the task, too. "Can I interest you in our members only rewards program?"

Rewards program? I was used to hearing about that

type of sales gimmick at coffee shops, and rightfully so. I freely admitted to my love of espresso, and those reward programs in the chain stores definitely came in handy…but knitting? How much yarn could one person use?

I daresay that a rewards program for either item or hobby might point to an addiction problem, dear hexed one.

Pearl wasn't one to talk such nonsense when she had to have her spot of warm cream three to four times daily.

It has been scientifically proven that a spot of warm cream is good for a familiar's overall health. Remember, Miss Lilura, I am no ordinary housecat with their rather commonplace dietary restrictions.

I decided to end this disagreement with Pearl and to also not push Julie Kirkham any more than we already had this morning. The story of Piper's grandmother would only get us so far before someone caught on to our ruse and started asking probing questions.

It wasn't long before Piper had a rather large bag of knitting purchases in her possession and a big smile on her face. Now this was what envy felt like, only I wanted to substitute her knitting purchases with a barista machine that could pump out a double shot of espresso. On second thought, especially after stepping outside, a caramel macchiato sounded divine. I'm pretty confident that the temperature had dropped a couple of degrees while we were inside.

"Who are Roger and Debbie Wilkes, and what do they have to do with Edgar's murder?" Piper asked immediately after we'd sidestepped a couple of other women entering the shop. I was still amazed by this new craze I was witnessing in regard to knitting. "Mrs. Kirkham was shaking so hard that I was afraid she'd stick herself with one of my new knitting needles."

My sweet Piper, I'd say it's more likely that our dear hexed one here might use that needle on the woman currently holding onto Mr. Emeric's arm. You should hold the bag with your other hand and keep all weapons out of reach.

For the first time this morning, I wasn't taken by surprise. I'd seen Knox and his little she-wolf the moment we'd stepped outside. Orwin was walking beside them, though his nose was practically inches from his phone.

"Lou and Piper, I'd like you to meet Vanessa Carlisle," Knox introduced, motioning for us all to continue walking. My problem with that scenario was that it was in the opposite direction of the café. "Vanessa, this is Lou and Piper. Somewhere around here is Piper's familiar—Pearl."

Our resident werewolf does have impeccable manners, does he not? Please tell Mrs. Carlisle that I'm pleased to make her acquaintance.

"There's a bakery a few shops down," Orwin said with a wave of his hand and without looking up from his phone. "You can get yourself a coffee there, Lou."

"It's nice to meet you, Vanessa," Piper greeted with her usual peppy smile, holding out a hand that was still bare. She'd yet to put back on her mittens since stepping outside. "How do you know our friend Knox? I wasn't aware that he had any friends around here. And Knox, weren't you supposed to be somewhere else?"

I could have hugged Piper, wanting to know that very question but afraid it would come across wrong. After all, Pearl had assumed that my problem with Knox was him having a she-wolf friend. That couldn't be further from the truth. I simply didn't like being lied to by my friends.

Keep telling yourself that, dear hexed one. One of us might actually believe it, if we don't think on it too hard.

Orwin barked out a laugh, but Knox and Vanessa incorrectly assumed that he was amused about something he'd read on his phone. I was more grateful in this moment that Knox couldn't hear Pearl than I was that the bakery up ahead would provide warmth and a much-needed caramel macchiato.

"I was at that specific location earlier this morning," Knox revealed while carefully watching his words in case someone overheard us. The five of us took up most of the sidewalk, so I stayed in front to lead the way while Knox and Piper carried on the discussion. I did find it unusual that Knox was so forthcoming when he usually preferred to remain quiet while taking in the conversation and surroundings. "I happened to see Vanessa and decided to touch base with her."

I slowed down my step so that we didn't come upon

the bakery too soon. The more information I had regarding this she-wolf before we were in an enclosed space would allow me to relax somewhat, which should be understandable to everyone involved.

I do agree that it is always wise to take precautions, dear hexed one.

A quick glance across the street still showed that the fortune teller's neon sign that designated whether or not the shop was open still had not been turned on. It appeared that those detectives really had taken Gracie Lynn into the station for questioning.

"I actually met Vanessa when I was following you from Washington to Pennsylvania all those months ago," Knox revealed, finally giving me an answer to my question. I still wasn't comfortable with having an outsider brought in on a case without having had a group discussion first. Did Vanessa know the entire truth about Knox? "She and her pack were kind enough to offer me a home, but I graciously turned her down due to my job."

I believe Mr. Emeric replied to your question, Miss Lilura. It was as if he was attuned to your thoughts and actually made an effort to put your mind at ease.

I could do without Pearl's commentary, so I didn't hesitate to open the glass door to the bakery. Maybe I'd even sneak her a spot of warm cream in a cup to divert her attention for a moment or two. Orwin was already mumbling about buying another blueberry scone while the others grabbed a private table in the back. A bit of privacy while standing in line for a beverage to give me back my sanity was just what the doctor ordered.

"I told the others I'd grab their drinks," Orwin said behind me, causing me to close my eyes in acceptance that my moment of bliss had evaporated just that quickly. "Pearl's right, you know. Your bad day started when you saw Vanessa, because you immediately jumped to conclusions. They're just friends. Nothing more."

"Knox should have called one of us the second he left the Booneville residence," I murmured, not wanting the older couple in front of us to hear our conversation. They were busy ordering those blueberry scones that Orwin had taken a liking to, so their attention was thankfully elsewhere. "Please just catch me up on the Wilkes. Debbie was Norma's partner? How did we miss that?"

I wasn't criticizing Orwin's research in the slightest. I'd had a hand in putting together the dossier, too. There had been no mention of Debbie Wilkes' name on any of the paperwork associated with the knitting store. I waited for Pearl to jump into the conversation, but there was nothing but silence from her.

"I should have rephrased my text to you," Orwin said, pushing up his black-rimmed glasses when he took a step forward to stand directly beside me. "Debbie wanted to be Norma's partner, especially since Norma had plans to travel after Edgar's retirement. The business emails that I'm reading through basically say that Debbie quit after Norma didn't hold up her end of a verbal agreement."

"You hacked into the knitting shop's email server?" I asked, wondering if Pearl wasn't right about the inevitable black van that was bound to show up in our rearview mirror. "Don't answer that. What does she-wolf—I mean, Vanessa—have to do with this case?"

It was our turn to give our order, so I waited for Orwin to relay what the others wanted before adding my own caramel macchiato. I shouldn't have gotten my hopes up, because the barista explained that they only served flavored coffee, but that I could walk down to the café to get my preferred beverage. Let's just say I ended up with an espresso once again.

"I could have sworn I sent those details to you in a text," Orwin said with a frown, lifting his phone and opening up his messages as we waited at the pickup counter for our drinks and his blueberry scone. "Hmmm. I guess I forgot to include that bit of interesting information."

"Interesting?" I asked, unable to stop myself from glancing at the table in the corner. Vanessa had chosen to sit next to Knox, who just so happened to be staring at me. His dark gaze was regarding me carefully, so I managed to force myself to give a half-smile in return. "I thought she was simply a casual acquaintance who Knox happened to look up since we were back in this area."

I do remember that Orwin and I had ventured this far north when we were traveling to find Piper, whom we had originally thought might be able to cure me of this hex. Unfortunately, we'd discovered that her gift didn't work on curses of this nature. I also had an inherent sense that this so-called interesting information wasn't going to brighten my day.

I'll explain this as delicately as I can, dear hexed one— the she-wolf claims that Edgar Booneville is her uncle. I'm going to need that spot of warm cream you offered.

Chapter Five

"**I** THINK YOU better start at the beginning," I said pointedly to Vanessa once we were all sitting down at the large table in the back of the bakery. It was technically two tables we'd pushed together, but it accommodated us comfortably while affording Pearl a small hiding place to enjoy her spot of warm cream. Unfortunately, eating and drinking was not something she could do while invisible. "Are you telling me that Edgar Booneville was a victim of lycanthropy?"

If that was truly the case, then we'd been going about this murder mystery all wrong. I hadn't been aware that mistletoe was poisonous to werewolves. Then again, I hadn't believed that Ammeline Letty Romilda was anything more than an urban legend.

I believe I might be in need of one of my own knock-knock jokes, dear hexed one.

Pearl didn't like surprises when it came to witchcraft or the supernatural. She believed her two thousand years on this earth provided her with a wealth of information, thereby granting to her a certain measure of superiority, basically sitting on a pedestal like most domestic cats expecting to be granted fealty by their humans.

Orwin gave me a pointed look that told me not to get Pearl started on being the superior species. I would have laughed if this were any other time, but we were faced with a dilemma where the supernatural realm was about to cross over into the lives of several humans. This type of situation was inherently dangerous for everyone involved.

"No," Vanessa answered with a sad smile that told me just how fond she was of her dearly departed uncle. "Uncle Edgar was entirely too human. My grandmother was human, also. She'd fallen in love with my grandfather, but he died soon after my father was born. Some vampires had gone rogue and were passing through town. They were eventually dealt with, but not before there was a casualty."

I can breathe a little easier, dear hexed one. No need for that knock-knock joke you seemed in such a hurry to tell me.

"And your grandmother then remarried?" Piper asked, shooting Orwin a smile when he'd set a packet of sugar next to her tea. "How did she manage to hide the fact that your father was a werewolf? You're bound to the curse of the full moon, right?"

Technically, the curse didn't take effect until the werewolf reached puberty. I understood where Piper was leading this conversation, and even I couldn't fathom how it was possible to keep such a secret from friends and family. Unless, of course, Edgar's mother had shared her husband's lycanthrope secret with her immediate family.

You might have just given me a touch of indigestion, Miss Lilura. I do hope that the late Mrs. Booneville hadn't been so careless with the lives of her husband and son.

"Yes, my father's line is bound by the curse," Vanessa answered, wrapping her hands around the cup of coffee. Knowing that it was rare for a lycanthrope's body temperature to run low, she'd done it more to give her hands something to do while sharing with us her family history than to keep them warm. "My grandmother succumbed to the will of my father's pack. Our leader believed that my father would be safer amongst that side of his family. A decision was made that my father would be with the pack on the week of the full moon, and an arrangement was made. Uncle Edgar had no idea that his brother was a lycanthrope, and it stayed that way until his recent untimely death."

I hadn't expected to feel so much sorrow for Vanessa as she shared her family history, but I couldn't even imagine the frustration she felt in having her hands tied when it came to the inherent need to become a predator in this instance. She was fighting her basic instinct to hunt and avenge a murder.

We cannot allow that to happen, Miss Lilura.

"I didn't know that Edgar Booneville was a relative of Vanessa's until I saw her walk into the family home this morning. On her way out, she caught my scent," Knox admitted, leaning back into his chair. "All Vanessa wants is justice, but this isn't pack business. For their safety, I suggested that she leave this in our hands. It's what we do, owning a private investigation firm and all. We will deal with the perpetrator."

Mr. Emeric's code of honor is shining through once again, dear hexed one.

That was Pearl's way of telling me that I shouldn't have jumped to conclusions about why Knox hadn't remained at the Booneville residence. I shot back my espresso to give me the strength to get through the remaining few minutes we'd need to gather information, wanting this case over with now more than ever. Humility was a bitter pill.

"Vanessa, do you know of anyone who would want to hurt your uncle?" Orwin asked, undoubtedly attuned with my thoughts seeing as he was sitting directly across from me. "We have several suspects, and most are on the list due to his profession. He recently retired, but I can only imagine not without making a few enemies over the years."

Who would have thought that contract law would attract so many foes?

"Gracie Lynn," Vanessa replied without hesitation. Her dark brown hair fell over her right shoulder as she continued to give us details. "She confronted Uncle Edgar at the diner last week, and she even made a threat on his life. That woman is no more witch than I am a vampire. She gathers her information from being in the right place at the right time. She keeps her ears open and reads people's body language well. She then drops hints as if she has a sixth sense, but it's all in how she words her sentences that keeps people on the fence on whether or not to believe she's the real thing."

I do like this she-wolf's sense of humor, Miss Lilura.

Orwin tapped the top of his phone, alerting me to the fact that he was using his new software to gather a brief synopsis of Gracie Lynn's background. The online search would no doubt be completed faster if Orwin established a link to his laptop, but his phone would have to do for now.

"Vanessa, that still doesn't explain how the poison got into Edgar's drink," I pointed out, not seeing how Gracie Lynn could have snuck into the Booneville residence on the day in question. "We know that your uncle didn't leave the house on Sunday from what was reported to the police."

Thank you to Mr. Cornelia, whose technological skills are splendid. Have you thought about why you are so obsessed with those little green men, alien hunter?

Pearl always managed to antagonize Orwin at the absolute worst time, but I had to admit that it was fun to watch his reaction. We really didn't have time to waste, though.

"Are you suggesting that Gracie Lynn somehow

managed to sneak into your uncle's house without anyone noticing? How could she have known when or if anyone would use that particular decanter?" I asked skeptically, not sure that Vanessa had thought through her theory. "You realize that Debbie Wilkes and her husband had just as much motive as the town's fortune teller, right?"

"Not only as much motive, but did you know that Roger Wilkes stopped by your uncle's estate the day he was poisoned?" Orwin inquired, tapping his phone once again. "He's already been questioned by the police, and even your aunt backed up his claim that the two of them spoke civilly about the verbal agreement made between Norma and Debbie. He was also nowhere near the library where the decanter was sitting."

"Debbie Wilkes might have been upset that Norma didn't want a partner, but the reason she quit was—"

"Incoming," Knox murmured, having lifted his coffee cup to cover up the fact that he was letting us know someone was approaching the table.

Oh, dear. We might have some explaining to do, dear hexed one.

"Vanessa, what are you doing here?"

The sudden appearance of Abigail Lincoln, Norma's much maligned daughter, had all of us sipping our drinks, waiting patiently to hear the upcoming exchange. I met Knox's gaze, which seemed somewhat apologetic over our circumstances. He knew very well that I didn't like to have my back to the door after my run-in with Ammeline, but Vanessa had taken the chair next to him. Telling her to move would have come across as oddly rude coming from a stranger.

That hasn't stopped you before, dear hexed one. Methinks that you didn't want our resident werewolf to get the wrong idea…or would it be the right idea you've tried to camouflage in vain?

It was a good thing that Pearl had finished her spot of warm cream, because I had a strong urge to knock it over. She might be Piper's familiar, but she treated me like an older sister would in these types of situations.

You can't slide one past me, dear hexed one. You secretly love that I consider you family.

"Abigail, these are my friends. They were just passing through and wanted to give me their condolences." Vanessa had been smart to keep the reason for our visit vague. "I told Aunt Norma that I was coming into town. I could have brought you something back."

"I appreciate that, but Mom wanted me to stop by the shop and make sure that Julie had things covered with the new shipment that arrived this morning." Abigail was a pretty woman in her forties, and it was clear from her red nose and bloodshot eyes that she'd had an emotional time of it as of late. Understandable, and her willingness to help her mother out went toward her character. "I see you told them about Mom's sale at the knitting shop."

Abigail was talking about Piper's large bag, which

she'd hung from the back of the chair.

"She did," Piper agreed, but gracefully managed to slip in our cover story so that it meshed with what we'd been telling everyone around town. "Although my grandmother actually met your mother at a knitting convention years ago. We're sorry for your loss."

"I appreciate that," Abigail said with a sad smile. "It was nice meeting all of you. Vanessa, are you heading back to the house? Patrick is waiting for me in the car and was going to drop me back off with Mom, but he really needs to go into work to tie up some loose ends."

I must admit that Mrs. Lincoln seems very genuine. My sweet Piper might need to slide her name down a slot or two on the suspect list. I couldn't imagine this woman wanting to kill her father.

"Of course," Vanessa replied automatically, scooting back her chair. She slung her purse over her shoulder, picking up her cup in the process. Surprisingly, she leaned down and kissed Knox on the cheek. "Knox, would you like to come with me? We can meet everyone else later for dinner after they're done shopping."

Oh, dear!

Orwin coughed discreetly, while Piper's blue eyes widened to the point that I was afraid she might actually lose an eyeball. I blamed Pearl for this, because she was the one who'd planted the idea in everyone's head that there was something more between Knox and me than friendship and our mutual adversary.

We all agree that thou doth protest too much, dear

hexed one. It is not a crime to want more than friendship from someone you admire.

It was a crime to strangle a familiar, though.

I find no humor in your vile thoughts whatsoever, dear hexed one.

"Sounds like a plan." Knox already had his seat out a bit from the table, so he didn't have to move it to stand up. "We'll catch up with all of you later this evening."

And that is what we call karma, my dearest colleagues.

I really tried not to roll my eyes. It wouldn't do for Knox to think my exasperation was due to him leaving with Vanessa.

"We'll walk you out," Piper said, picking up her tea with the intention of meeting Patrick. Orwin had already grabbed the bag with her knitting purchases, all the while having his nose practically pressed to his phone screen. He must have gotten a hit on Gracie Lynn. I'd be interested to know the woman's backstory. Right now, we all needed to regroup. "I have to say that your mother's store is…"

I remained at the table, though I did get up so that I could switch seats. Facing the front of the shop so that I could see who was coming and going had me a bit more comfortable. Piper and Orwin would be back so that we could talk over strategy. For some reason, Vanessa didn't believe that Roger or Debbie Wilkes had anything to do with Edgar's death. I believed those email exchanges regarding the verbal agreement for Debbie to become partner still needed to be explored.

I'd just taken the seat that Piper had vacated when I sensed someone approaching, yet the slight hum of electricity I always felt when Knox was near told me that he'd returned.

"Do we need to talk about this?" The way Knox phrased the question had me wishing that I hadn't had that second round of double espresso. "Honestly, I never thought I'd run into Vanessa again, and I certainly didn't know her background."

"It's fine," I replied, trying not to grimace as I sounded like one of those memes on social media that Orwin was always showing me. "I'm relieved she doesn't know about us. I mean, not us, but the source of our hexes. I don't—"

Knox leaned over the table and wrapped his large hand around mine. I'd like to go on record that I believed myself to be the most rational woman on the face of the planet. I never panicked when the walls were closing in, and I handled myself with grace when backed into a corner. Once again, I'm putting all blame on the fact that I had a second round of a double shot espresso.

"I would never share your story with someone else," Knox replied genuinely, keeping his tone low so that this conversation remained between us. His golden gaze was focused solely on me, waiting for my reaction. "I hope you know that."

It's a bit hot in here, isn't it? I'm relatively sure that the heat between the two of you just baked up another batch of those blueberry scones that Mr. Cornelia fancies.

"Knox, keep in touch throughout the day," Piper said, having been close on Pearl's heels, but not close enough that she'd heard what Pearl had said. Piper hooked her bag from the knitting shop on the side of the chair again before setting her tea back down. "See? I told you that Lou wouldn't throw away your coffee."

The fact that I hadn't noticed that Knox left his coffee behind told me that I was off my game. It was a good thing that I had done a proximity spell to alert me if Ammeline was within a hundred miles of my location. At the rate I was going today, she could have been the one to walk up to the table without me even realizing it…and if Pearl mentioned that aloud so that Piper could overhear, I wasn't going to be responsible for my actions.

Duly noted, dear hexed one.

"I'll keep in touch, and you do the same," Knox agreed, answering Piper while doing that annoying thing where he studied my reaction. My hand felt rather cold after he reached for his coffee and turned on the heels of his rugged military boots. He'd stored away his favorite brown leather jacket for a winter one that was lined with shearling, but the coat still seemed to have been handmade just for the width of his shoulders. "Piper, I could use a scarf to go with this jacket."

Piper beamed and shot me a satisfied smile that all but promised every single one of us would be wearing knitted accessories after the holidays. Oh, I was starting to wish for the New Year to be rung in fast so that this one was a thing of the past.

Trust me, we'll have those knitted accessories as a reminder.

"You'll thank me when the temperature turns colder," Piper warned us, pushing a chair out with her boot when Orwin finally returned, giving Knox a nod as they passed each other. "Orwin, let me read through the email exchange between Mrs. Wilkes and Mrs. Booneville. Maybe I can find a reason to knock Mrs. Wilkes off the suspect list."

"Well, we're going to need to add another," Orwin replied grimly, shooting a glance over his shoulder. "While all of you were talking to Vanessa, I did some additional research on her father. Did you catch what she said about Edgar not knowing about his brother's werewolf curse, and that it stayed that way until his death?"

We need to warn Mr. Emeric of this revelation, dear colleagues.

I had to stop myself from lunging out of my seat to prevent Knox from going with Vanessa. Orwin had just pointed out something vital that we'd overlooked during the conversation, and we'd all missed it.

That we did, dear hexed one. Just to clarify, alien hunter, are you saying that we now have to add an entire pack of werewolves to the suspect list? I'm not so sure that my sweet Piper's app has the empty spaces for that many names. This is quite the dilemma.

Chapter Six

"**A**RE YOU SURE that Orwin should have gone to bail out Gracie Lynn?" Piper asked, biting her lower lip in worry. We'd stored her knitting purchases in the Jeep before making our way to the boutique that was currently having a thirty percent off sale. It also helped that the owner of the boutique played bridge every Thursday night with the Boonevilles. There was bound to be some chin-wagging going on over there. "I don't mean that, obviously. She was just taken in for questioning, but you know what I mean. Besides, I'm not sure what he could say to make her believe a stranger would show up to give her a ride back to town."

I believe the alien hunter mentioned the "desperate love route", where he needed a reading ASAP to see what happens in his immediate future. He was thinking that he should say he saw her being led out of her shop by police just as he was racing to her for insight. In his frantic need for a reading, he followed her to see if he could help.

"Yeah, I'm not so sure that's the route he should have chosen, either," I muttered, lifting my scarf a bit so that the wind didn't travel inside my jacket. We now had both Orwin and Knox to worry about, and it wasn't even lunchtime. "The last thing we need is for the tables to be turned, leaving us to be the ones bailing him out for stalking."

Oh, I do love when you show your sense of humor, dear hexed one.

"I like it better when we're all together, have a short suspect list, and we're able to solve the case in a day." Piper and I passed the chocolate shop, although this time there was a snowman instead of an elf holding up samples for passersby to take one from the tray. I'm pretty sure the change in costume had to do with the falling temperatures. "Maybe Pearl should have gone with him."

"We might need her here with us if Orwin calls and tells us that Gracie Lynn had nothing to do with Edgar's murder," I reminded her, doing my best to resist temptation. No chocolate for me until I'd had a proper lunch, which wouldn't be until after we visited a few more shops. "I don't want to be caught unaware if we're suddenly surrounded by a pack of werewolves, although they haven't dealt with adversaries like us. We are more than capable of defending ourselves."

Good point, dear hexed one. All I am getting a whiff of is that tantalizing chocolate. It does leave me wanting another spot of warm cream. On a side note, in order to put your mind at ease, Mr. Emeric is also more than capable of taking care of himself in stressful situations, especially when it comes to other werewolves. I'm sure that he is more than a match for her pack's alpha. In fact, I'm fairly sure our wolfman could eviscerate their entire enclave.

"If we discard the werewolf pack as suspects, we're left with Gracie Lynn, the wife, and the Wilkes as to who had motive," Piper pointed out, not resisting temptation. As a matter of fact, she'd grabbed two chocolate candy canes and handed me one. I'm pretty sure she did so in order to ensure that she wasn't the only one to gain a couple of pounds this holiday season. "Unless we add in the daughter and son-in-law, which we kind of ruled out."

I was beginning to wonder if that was a mistake. Our number one rule was that we shouldn't allow our opinions to cloud our judgement. Knox really didn't know Vanessa, yet he'd gone with her to the house that was still the scene of a crime.

"Technically, we only ruled out Abigail," I reminded her, deciding that I needed a bit of comfort right now. I plopped the entire chocolate candy cane into my mouth and immediately tried not to melt along with it after it landed on my tongue. What in the world did they do different in that shop? I wasn't comforted in the least, but I did feel marginally better in that I could now face whatever decided to land in front of us. "And that was due to the woman's sweet disposition, which could be an act. We need to keep her on the list until we're absolutely positive she didn't have anything to do with her father's murder."

"Cynic," Piper exclaimed before Pearl could, who'd gone unusually silent.

"Pearl?"

"I hate when she does that," Piper murmured, licking her fingers before putting her mittens back on. She came to a stop in front of the display window for Go Out In Style. Sure enough, the place was packed for the thirty percent off sale. "Gracie Lynn had to have overheard the business owner making plans for this sale, right? I mean, we've already established that she's not a true witch."

Piper had pretty much put a question mark on the end of her sentence. Her wariness went to show just how easy it was to convince others to believe in something that wasn't true.

"Go on in and speak with the owner," I prompted her, pulling my cell phone out of my coat pocket. "I want to touch base with Knox."

I waited for Pearl to remind me that Orwin had already conveyed that specific warning before leaving town, but she was still nowhere to be heard. Piper frowned, not happy that her familiar had chosen to disappear while already invisible. It was a feat, and Pearl had done it with ease.

"We should probably check your bag of yarn when Orwin gets back to town with the Jeep," I said with a smile that I wasn't able to stop. The thought of Pearl unraveling and shredding those skeins of yarn was quite comical. Piper's reaction? Not so much. "Sorry. I couldn't resist. Anyway, go on inside. I'll only be a minute."

I didn't waste time after Piper walked inside the crowded boutique. Placing the call to Knox took mere seconds, but it was clear by the fifth ring that he wasn't going to answer. I didn't bother to leave a message. I'd hear from him soon enough. He would see that I tried to contact him and touch base with me when he had a moment to himself.

In the meantime, Piper and I would continue to investigate this case as if it were any other. Before I could reach for the door, though, I caught sight of a man standing in front of Gracie Lynn's storefront. He was looking over his shoulder as he slid the key into the lock.

Who was he, and what was he doing entering Gracie Lynn's shop? Clearly, he had a key. It wasn't as if he were breaking and entering, but I couldn't pass up the opportunity to speak with him about the owner. Maybe he could shed light on this whole curse rumor thing that was going around.

A quick glance inside the boutique revealed that Piper had yet to make her way up to the back of the shop. I held up a finger that I was going to be a few more minutes before quickly making my way down the sidewalk and past the Four-Leaf Clover. I fought the urge to knock on the entrance to Gracie Lynn's studio, having already decided that I would feign surprise that she wasn't inside. Still, a bit of uneasiness swept through me as my hand closed over the doorknob of the old-fashioned style handle.

The inside of the shop was much as I'd imagined it to be, having witnessed many stores such as these owned by psychics and voodoo priestesses. Some of those individuals were the real deal, actual hedge witches dabbling on the edge of witchcraft, while some were just very good at reading people. Either way, the vibe was always the same—mysterious with an ominous energy that contained a bit of hope. It was all very contradictory.

A touch of incense hung in the air of the small waiting room filled with comfortable seats and brochures on what services were offered by Gracie Lynn. There were multiple displays of items for sale, such as tarot cards, meditation books, and various crystals. Jewelry was the centerpiece, labeling some for healing, good fortune, and even bracelets that attracted love.

There was a small coffee and tea area set up on a back table for those who were forced to wait for their appointment. A Keurig was positioned next to a rotating holder of numerous pods offering various eclectic samples. Had I not still been humming from those double shot espressos, I would have been tempted to have myself a cup.

What, or better yet, who I didn't notice was the man who'd entered using a key.

He had to have heard the bell chiming above the

door, yet there was complete silence coming from behind the multiple strings of gaudy purple beads. I'm not sure why fortune tellers always hung beaded curtains in doorways to their private reading room, but they certainly seemed to be the staple.

I'd evened out my breathing as I remained standing just inside the door, listening intently for any sound coming from behind those beads. Places like this didn't have hidden doors, so I was ninety-nine percent confident that the man was standing on the opposite side of the decorated curtain. I didn't have time for games, and I had the upper hand with my inherent ability of telekinesis.

"Gracie Lynn?" I called out, feigning my ignorance of her absence. Just in case the man was peering through the vast amount of purple beads, I walked over to the bracelets and began looking through them. "I'm here for my appointment."

The slightest sound of someone shifting their weight prompted the hardwood floor to squeak before once again settling into silence. Little by little, the uneasy sensation of being watched returned tenfold.

Just what game was this man playing?

Well, I didn't want to be a participating player. There was a very easy way to draw out the host, so I casually flicked my wrist. The stack of Styrofoam cups that were on the edge of the coffee and tea table abruptly tipped over, falling to the floor and knocking the strings of beads until they shifted back and forth to reveal the man who had been watching me since I'd walked in the front door.

"Oh, hi," I called out as I feigned alarm at the sudden noise. "I think you knocked those over."

"I'm not sure what happened," the man replied, stepping out from behind the strings of beads as if that had been his intention all along. The deep frown lines in his forehead displayed his confusion as to how the cups got knocked over to begin with, but that didn't stop him from picking them up and setting them back on the table. "Um, the shop is closed. If you had an appointment with Ms. Hauver, you'll have to reschedule."

"Closed?" I asked with feigned surprise. I even took my phone out of my coat pocket for added effect, checking for messages. "That's odd. I didn't get a call from Gracie Lynn. She usually lets me know if we need to reschedule. Are you her husband? I didn't even know she was married."

Gracie Lynn Hauver wasn't married, at least according to Orwin's initial research. My instinct was telling me that the man standing next to the coffee and tea station was her landlord, especially given that he wasn't wearing a winter coat. He'd come from somewhere close, and he'd obviously known that she wasn't inside conducting readings.

"Husband?" the man asked in surprise. He palmed his keys, looking me over as if just now realizing that I wasn't a local. Really, though, how many locals came in for a reading? "I'm not married to Ms. Hauver. She's my tenant. My name is Roy Eisaman. I was, um, just checking on some things while she's out of town."

"You make it sound like she won't be back anytime soon."

It hit me that Roy might have been taking a look inside the shop to see if Gracie Lynn had been packing up her things to move to another site. Given that she was supposed to be moved out in two weeks, there wasn't a box in sight.

"You'll have to take that up with her," Roy exclaimed, clearly done speaking with me. He even motioned toward the door that I should leave. "Have a good day, miss."

There was another way to play this situation, although it did risk blowing our cover story. Roy seemed like a pretty tight-lipped kind of guy, though. I decided to take the chance that he didn't fall in line with the gossip train around this town.

"You got me, Mr. Eisaman," I exclaimed, holding up my hands in surrender. "My friend and I are actually in town doing an exclusive on Edgar Booneville's murder. A source at the state police told me that Gracie Lynn Hauver was a suspect, and I was hoping to speak with her...maybe even get a quote for tomorrow's paper. Seeing as you are her landlord, who better to talk to in her place? Do you think your tenant is capable of murder?"

Roy was definitely taken aback by the sudden turn in this situation, but I'd definitely baited him…hook, line, and sinker.

"Someone told you about Gracie Lynn's argument with Edgar over at the diner last week, didn't they?" Roy wiped his nose with the back of his hand, darting his gaze toward the door in a bit of paranoia. He then pointed toward the ceiling, causing me to look up at a vent. "I heard her chanting that night, you know. I told the police. I don't know how she did it, but that woman is the reason Edgar is dead. No one can tell me different, either."

"What did Gracie Lynn say during that chant?" I asked, wanting more specifics. There were a lot of incantations that could be done with dire consequences, even by hedge witches. There were some powerful spells that even a mere human could cast with the right ingredients. One shouldn't mess with dark magic, and that included those born into the craft. "Do you remember?"

"No," Roy replied with a shake of his head. He pursed his lips, as if simply being in this shop could get him cursed. If only he knew that a Lich Queen walked among us, he wouldn't even step one foot outside of his house. It was best not to feed into his fear, and I needed to figure out a way to ease his concern about the unknown. "I only know that she sounded like those witches on that Netflix show. The police believe me, you know. That's why Ms. Hauver isn't here. They took her in for questioning."

"My source at the police station didn't tell me that," I confessed with a shrug. I did hold up my phone as if I had some information that he'd like to know. "The other suspect was questioned today, though. My source seemed pretty confident that the evidence was pointing in her direction."

"Her?" Roy didn't seem to appreciate that the police were looking at someone other than Gracie Lynn. "What other suspect? The police couldn't possibly believe that Norma killed Edgar, do they? That's preposterous!"

"Oh, my source didn't give me a name," I said with an innocent blink. My phone happened to vibrate with an incoming message, so I used that as an excuse to leave. "I have to take this, but I appreciate you talking to me. I promise to leave your name out of the article."

I quickly left, hopefully planting a seed of doubt in Roy's mind. It wouldn't do to have the residents of this town believing in spells and witchcraft. The bitter cold hit me in the face, along with a few flurries. What I hadn't expected was for Pearl to make a sudden appearance. All I can say was that it was a good thing there were slick spots here and there on the sidewalk, because I stumbled over my own Ugg boots at her abrupt arrival.

"You have to stop doing that," I muttered in disbelief, pasting a smile on my face as I passed by a mother who was attempting to tug her toddler away from running after the snowman across the street. "One of these times I'm going to keel over from a heart attack."

There's still a chance that could happen after you hear what I discovered after following one son-in-law into the real estate office down the road. I'll have you know my eyesight is as keen as ever, dear hexed one.

I continued to walk back toward the boutique while waiting for Pearl to fill me in, but she was in one of those moods where she liked to be prompted to reveal the details.

Don't rain on my holiday parade, Miss Lilura. I, too, contribute to these mysteries of ours.

"I know you do," I replied softly, having finally arrived back at the boutique. It was still quite crowded, so it was doubtful that Piper had been able to have a private word with the owner. "Spill it. You mentioned son-in-law. Does this have to do with Patrick Lincoln?"

It certainly does.

"Hey," Piper called out, holding up what looked to be a burnt orange cardigan sweater. It wasn't surprising, given her obsession with anything to do with pumpkins. "If I get a handle on those hats, scarves, and mittens, I bet I could make a killer cardigan."

We were just talking about killers, my sweet Piper. You see, you'll want to move one Mr. Patrick Lincoln up in the suspect pool on your app. While we were well aware from Mr. Cornelia's research that Mr. Lincoln is a lawyer, we did not know that he has secretly been planning to open up an office right here in Covered Bridge, North Dakota.

Chapter Seven

*T*HERE ARE QUITE *a lot of moving pieces in this murder mystery, dear hexed one.*

There were a lot of suspects to sift through, and Orwin deciding to bail the town's fortune teller out of jail was delaying the final reveal. Okay, he'd only gone to pick her up, not technically fork up some money to spring her from a jail cell. That decision had still taken away our capability of discarding suspects just by standing next to them.

Has the alien hunter texted back?

"No," I murmured after passing the same mother who'd been chasing her after her son. It appeared that he'd successfully made it to the snowman, if the smeared chocolate around his mouth was anything to go by. "We should hear from him soon, though."

Piper and I had decided to split up so that she could talk to the boutique owner who played bridge with the Boonevilles every Thursday, while I took a short stroll to the real estate office on the other side of the street. I understood why Orwin thought it best to follow Gracie

Lynn to the police station. She'd been our number one suspect, but we also knew how quickly that could change.

As quick as the drop of a snow flurry, Miss Lilura. Speaking of which, we shall have to take a moment to enjoy this winter wonderland. I do believe I see St. Nick taking his seat. I do not have to ask what it is you want for Christmas, so you'll have to come up with a more achievable present.

"You know that a snow flurry takes forever to land, right?"

We crossed the cobblestone intersection by ourselves, although only I was visible. Most of the shops were behind us, whereas the real estate office and some of the related businesses were down on this end of town. This allowed me to speak freely, as I still found it hard to talk with Pearl only using my thoughts.

Not in a blizzard, dear hexed one. Those fluffy white flakes fall at a rapid pace with those gusts of winds. I fear that this murder mystery has us smackdab in the middle of one, what with all these not-so-obvious suspects popping up left and right.

"Let's see if we can't take a name off that list," I suggested, thinking back to what Pearl said about Patrick. We put a lot of stock into the online research we do before arriving at a crime scene, but what if Patrick's decision to move hadn't been a secret? For all we knew, the family had discussed this thoroughly before Edgar's murder. "I'll try and—"

Patrick Lincoln stepped out of the realtor's office, buttoning his black wool dress coat. He was in his mid-forties, though he did have a receding hairline. The rimless glasses made him appear a little older, but maybe that was a good thing in his profession.

"Excuse me," Patrick said without really looking at up as he slipped past on the sidewalk.

I suppose I can give him a pass since he remembered his manners. I didn't particularly care for his dismissive attitude, but that doesn't make one a killer.

I'd hoped to have a word with Patrick, but his rushed exit told me that now wasn't the time. He had been a bit dismissive, and I highly doubted that I would have gotten any details out of him.

"May I help you?"

I'd turned to watch Patrick walk back to his black Mercedes, understanding exactly where Esther and Sandra had been coming from when they'd mentioned what type of vehicle he drove. This town didn't have a lot of BMWs or Mercedes driving up and down Main Street. The high-pitched voice came from an older woman who couldn't have been taller than five feet. Her blond hair was piled high on top her head, and I'm pretty sure that there were at least two pencils in that beehive.

Takes me back to the 1950s. I do miss my Elvis.

"Um, hi. My name is Lou," I replied, quickly figuring out which story would garner me the most information. The fact that Pearl knew Elvis had me stumbling a bit. "My friend and I are in town to do some Christmas shopping, and I overheard someone mention that a storefront might be available to rent at the beginning of the year."

"Oh, you must be talking about Spiritual Readings & More," the woman replied, nodding toward the other side of the street while locking up her own storefront. She finished up, dropping her keys in her purse before holding out her hand. "My name is Susan Hatley. What kind of shop were you thinking of opening? The space won't be ready for show until the first of January, but we can certainly go ahead and set up an appointment. Does nine o'clock on the first sound good to you? I have someone else who is scheduled for a showing at eight o'clock."

Ms. Hatley is very proficient at her job, is she not? I do so like the go-getter type.

"If you could just let me know the price of rent, I'll then be able to pass it on to my friend," I said, keeping things vague. I had no idea if Susan Hatley was possibly friends with Roy Eisaman. "She keeps talking about opening up a craft store. Not knitting, of course. She saw that you had one of those already."

"Oh, yes," Susan exclaimed, reaching into her coat pocket to pull out a pair of gloves. It didn't surprise me to see that they had been knitted in cream-colored yarn. "Knitting has made a comeback, and Norma's shop has just been making a killing."

Our little Ms. Hatley might be a go-getter, but she speaks before thinking. She should work on that.

The little squeak that came out of Susan's mouth revealed that she'd heard her own words. She rested one of those knitted mittens on her cheek in dismay. Seeing her eyes dart to where Patrick had been parked was the perfect opening in the conversation for me to finally step in.

"That was Patrick Lincoln, wasn't it?" I said with a sympathetic tilt of my head. "Don't feel bad. He's long gone. I heard about what happened to Mrs. Booneville's husband. It's just horrible, so you can imagine my surprise when I saw her son-in-law walking out of your office."

"Patrick is a good boy," Susan shared, seemingly feeling a bit better that I hadn't taken offense to her slip. It didn't take long for her to go from relief to full-on suspicion. "You aren't from here. How do you know Patrick?"

"I'm actually friends with Vanessa Carlisle," I explained, wondering how my nose hadn't frozen off yet. The random flurries were beginning to turn into a snow globe-type burst, but it was just enough to have the children in town square giggling and cheering in delight. "We're having dinner with her later this evening, but my friend and I thought we'd get some shopping in while the sales were still going on."

Quick thinking, dear hexed one. You are at the top of your game right now, aren't you?

"I feel so bad for Norma, but she's going to be so happy to know that Patrick finally signed the lease," Susan said, having no idea she was helping with our investigation. "They've been talking about it for a while now, but you probably already know that. It was supposed to have been a birthday surprise for Abigail, but now…well, I guess there isn't any need to wait, now is there? Life reminds us daily that it can end in the blink of an eye. We shouldn't waste precious minutes of happiness when they're ours to take."

Not only do I like Ms. Hatley's hairstyle, I love her outlook on life. You should take notes, dear hexed one.

"None of us could believe it when we heard that Mr. Booneville had been murdered." I turned as if I was going to walk back toward town square, hoping that Susan would fall into step. She did, and I was able to keep the conversation going in the direction I needed to gather more information. Pearl wanted me to take notes about not wasting time, and I couldn't agree more. I wanted this case solved and allow everyone the chance to enjoy a nice and relaxing holiday for once. "It feels odd to be Christmas shopping, but the world doesn't stop turning, does it?"

"No, it doesn't," Susan replied, pulling up the hood on the back of her winter coat. She adjusted her oversized purse as we continued down the sidewalk.

"Poor Norma. I'm sure she'll try to have Edgar's service this weekend, but the holidays will never be the same, will they? I'm heading home soon to bake her a casserole. The bridge club devised a meal plan, and today is my turn. I know this sounds horrible, but I wouldn't eat anything that anyone brought me if my husband had been poisoned."

Ms. Hatley does have a valid point. I'd be having the alien hunter test my spot of warm cream if you happened to be poisoned, dear hexed one.

"I heard the police took a woman in for questioning," I said, wanting to know what Susan's thoughts were on Gracie Lynn's involvement. "I believe it had something to do with her threatening Mr. Booneville's life in the middle of the diner. At least, that's what I overheard in one of the shops."

"You're talking about Gracie Lynn." Susan slowed her steps when we came to the cobblestone path that went directly from the sidewalk to town square. It was coming up on lunchtime, and the children were lining up to visit good ol' St. Nick. "That is the shop owner who is vacating her space in two weeks. She claims that she had an addendum in her contract to extend her lease, but she misunderstood the fine print. She wasn't happy that Edgar didn't think she'd stand a chance in court. Obviously, she shouldn't have caused a scene at the diner, but that woman doesn't have a mean bone in her body. I don't believe for a second that she poisoned

Edgar. Hold this."

What is with the people of this town? Just when I believe they have the most modest sense of etiquette, they go and do something rude.

Susan basically shoved her oversized purse in my arms while she dug through it with her knitted gloves, pulling out a business card and pen. She scribbled something on it before taking back her purse, though I wasn't certain her handwriting would be legible. Who wrote while wearing gloves?

Apparently, the throwback to the 1950s. For the record, she doesn't deserve that hairstyle.

"That is the monthly rent on a year's lease for the storefront," Susan said, shoving her pen into her beehive. She flashed me a harried smile. "I'm off to show someone a house before making that casserole, but do keep in touch!"

It was clear that Susan had a bit too much on her plate, and she definitely wasn't taking her own advice about enjoying the time given to her. Although, I changed my mind once I glanced down at the back of the business card in my hand. That was a hefty monthly rent. Good ol' Susan must be rolling in the commissions.

Speaking of rolling, you might want to—

A big fluffy snowball came out of nowhere, covering half my face after the rest exploded all over my scarf and jacket. I stood there in shock, blinking rapidly to clear my sight. The tricky thing about telekinesis was that it only came in handy when I was prepared. I heard giggling and falsetto voices of several boys and girls blaming one another, with a few of them yelling out apologies as they continued with their snowball fight.

I did try to warn you, dear hexed one.

I wasn't sure if Pearl was talking about the snowball or the fact that Knox stood in front of me with that charming crooked smile of his.

"Playing without me?"

Oh, my heavens! Have we discussed flirting, Miss Lilura?

Chapter Eight

"LET'S GO INSIDE the diner and get you warmed up," Knox said, stepping forward and using his thumb to wipe away the snow that was still attached to my eyelashes. "I leave you alone for an hour and you're getting into snowball fights with the local kids."

Please tell Mr. Emeric that he's stealing my line. It's rude to borrow without permission.

"What can I say?" I replied wryly, tucking the business card in my pocket. The snow that had tucked in behind my scarf was starting to melt against my neck. "I thought I'd start their training young."

You're quick on your feet after that hit, dear hexed one. It's good to know that you haven't lost your touch.

"That was quite the hit," Piper interjected, coming up behind Knox. Her blue eyes were filled with laughter. Not even a smidge of concern was shown that the entire left side of my face was still covered with snow. "I tried to call out to you, but you couldn't hear me over the caroling. Knox, aren't you supposed to be over at the Boonevilles?"

Wolves. They get so easily distracted, don't they?

"About that," Knox said with caution, taking a look around before gesturing toward the diner. "Let's go and have an early lunch. Even though there are a lot of out-of-towners, I'd rather not draw attention to ourselves by standing around talking about an unsolved murder."

I wasn't going to argue about walking into a warm place for more than five minutes. Uncontrollable shivers were beginning to set in as the snow had pretty much melted into very cold water against my skin. Piper led the way, a small bag from the boutique swinging in her hand.

Maybe my sweet Piper has moved on from the knitting craze. You know, it's my experience that those fads don't last for long.

"Keep telling yourself that," I muttered, having no doubt that we'd be wearing matching hats come Christmas morning. "I think you're becoming more optimistic in your old age, Pearl."

"I definitely don't want to know what the two of you are talking about, do I?" Knox inquired, falling into step beside me as we crossed the street.

"Not if you want to end up with a knitted hat that includes dog ears," I replied with a smile, grateful that Pearl and I weren't the only ones who were going to be on the receiving end of Piper's gift exchange. "Would you please grab me a coffee? I'm going to use the restroom to try and dry out."

We'd finally reached the diner, and the warmth of the heat blowing down from above near the door was a welcome respite. I stood there a moment longer while Piper picked us out a table. The delicious remnant scent of bacon still hung in the air, but even I didn't need Knox's sense of smell to breathe in the mouthwatering coffee aroma.

One would have thought you had enough caffeine running through your veins by now, but your lack of reaction when hit in the face with a snowball says otherwise. Oh, look! My sweet Piper was able to get us a table in the back. I'll have another spot of warm cream, dear hexed one, along with a tuna sandwich, hold the bread. I have a feeling I might need it after hearing what our resident werewolf has to say.

I, too, wanted to hear what had Knox leaving the Booneville residence to return to town, but I first had to dry off. The restroom was off to the side, so I didn't waste time. Thankfully, the diner had installed one of those powerful air dryers. By the time I was done, I was warmer than Knox on a good day, though my hair now had a bit of static to it.

That's debatable, dear hexed one. A werewolf's internal temperature runs near a hundred and four degrees.

"Okay," I said with a renewed sense of purpose after hanging my winter coat on the back of my chair. I kept the scarf around my neck now that it was dry and warm, sliding into the chair next to Knox. We were both facing the door, which made my disposition even sunnier. "Is this about Patrick?"

"Patrick?" Knox slid the sugar over my way, looking a bit perplexed. Whatever information he'd gleaned at the house hadn't been about Patrick Lincoln. "What did you find out about the son-in-law?"

"Pearl was the one who actually realized something was amiss when she saw him walk into the realtor's office down the street." I added the two packets of sugar and stirred in a bit of cream, not surprised when my stomach grumbled. Those two small bits of chocolate weren't nearly enough to fill me up. "I just followed up on the lead."

I do so appreciate you giving me credit where credit is due.

"And?" Piper asked, dipping a tea bag into a cup of hot water. She'd removed all of her winter outerwear, only leaving on her hat. Her blonde ponytail was just as perfect as when we'd vacated the RV. I couldn't say the same about mine, especially when some of the strands had gotten wet from getting hit in the face with a snowball and then blown dry by a wall-mounted hand dryer. "What did you find out about Patrick?"

"Susan Hatley made it seem that Norma already knew about Patrick signing a lease for an office here in town," I said, setting down my spoon so that the wet end rested on a used sugar packet. "It was supposed to have been a surprise for Abigail, but then her father was murdered."

Death does tend to ruin the entire surprise aspect, dear hexed one.

"So there goes Patrick's motive for killing his father-in-law." Piper reached behind her, collecting her cell phone. She entered a long string of numbers which allowed her to access that special murder app of hers. "Patrick and Abigail moving back to town to be closer to her parents doesn't scream guilty party, and they also weren't the beneficiary of Edgar's life insurance policy."

My sweet Piper has become a tad bit paranoid after being around the alien hunter this past year. How do you remember all those numbers, my sweet?

"It's called being cautious," Piper replied without pause. "And I'm not the one who decided to tell Orwin that there was evidence of alien life in the pyramids. You realize that you have Orwin mapping out a trip to Egypt to check that out, right?"

Pearl remained suspiciously quiet, so much so that we all stopped to look at one another. I'd always maintained that Piper's familiar was a shrewd one. Her two thousand years had bestowed upon her more knowledge than we could ever hope to gain in our short lifespans. A part of me was in awe at her ability to work a situation.

"If you wanted to go back to Egypt, all you had to do was tell me," Piper said with a frown. I hid a smile at her protectiveness over Orwin. "Pearl, are there depictions that prove UFOs exist in those pyramids or were you just pulling a fast one on Orwin to get him to take you back to Egypt?"

I do believe my charge is upset with my tactics, dear hexed one.

"Better fix it," I muttered behind my coffee cup, sharing an amused glance with Knox.

He couldn't hear Pearl, but he definitely got the gist of the conversation. I didn't want to ponder why I was more relaxed with him here with us than at the Booneville residence. Something had clearly happened for him to want to discuss it in person, but my stomach was beginning to grumble and we needed a break from all the walking around town. Besides, there were only so many snowballs to the face I could take without waging an all-out war on the children. I'm sure that would be frowned upon by the parents of my fellow combatants.

My sweet Piper, you know how I feel about lying. I value loyalty above all else, and the alien hunter has become like family…in the "odd one in the bunch" kind of way. You can rest assured there are signs pointing in the direction of alien life, though no one is certain. Isn't that the fun of exploration, darling?

"Piper, you and I both know that Orwin loves debating with Pearl," I interjected when I saw signs that the waitress was headed our way. "Honestly, a vacation to explore the pyramids sounds good right about now."

I somehow depressed myself a tad bit, because it was highly doubtful that I would ever be able to go on vacation. The length of time between premonitions wasn't long enough, and my need for justice was too strong to let one slide by without trying to either save a life or put their killer behind bars.

Well, you certainly know how to ruin a carefree moment, Miss Lilura. Knock-knock.

I was saved from answering that door when the waitress finally stood at our table, ready to take our lunch order. Being reminded of my current lot in life had my appetite fading, so I ordered a cup of chicken noodle soup. It would help keep me warm when Piper and I headed back out to visit some other shops.

"What happened with the boutique owner?" I asked Piper once the waitress had left to go and put in our order. I had already scanned the patrons in the diner to see if I recognized anyone. Esther and Sandra weren't among them, and neither was Roy Eisaman. The landlord's absence was a relief. "Did she have anything to say about the Boonevilles?"

"We're going to have to go back," Piper said before taking a sip of her tea. She'd asked the waitress if we could have the small ceramic cream dispenser warmed up in the microwave for exactly twenty-one seconds. Had we been in a big city, the waitress wouldn't have thought anything of such a request. This place was another matter altogether, but the waitress was a bit too busy to kibitz about it. "That flash sale had customers filing in there in droves. She was too busy for me to ask her anything."

The waitress isn't a cat person, either. There wasn't one

strand of cat hair on her uniform. I notice these things, dear hexed one.

"You're definitely going to want to go back to the boutique after we're done having lunch," Knox said, still leaning back in his chair. He was resting his right forearm on the table so that he could hold his coffee. His golden eyes hinted that he had a secret, and it proved to be a doozy. "What's her name again?"

"Iris Drummond." Piper didn't even look up from typing her notes into the app. "She and her husband, Bill, are regulars at the Thursday night card games."

"Why do you ask?" I inquired, waiting for the twist in this mystery. There was usually a curveball thrown at us, and I doubted this case would be an exception. "Was Iris' name brought up at the house?"

"No," Knox answered as he rubbed the five o'clock shadow along his jawline. "But you might want to ask good ol' Iris why someone would want Norma Booneville dead."

Oh, I could definitely use that spot of warm cream right about now. Is our wolfman saying that Mr. Booneville was not the intended target?

I could understand why Pearl would word her question like that. Knox had spoken so casually that it took a moment for me to digest his words. Even Piper's hand hovered over her phone as if she wasn't quite sure she'd heard him correctly.

"You're going to want to start at the beginning," I urged, coming to the conclusion that we'd been working this case all wrong. "Why do you think someone was after Norma and not her husband?"

"Vanessa introduced me to Norma, as well as those close family members and friends who were visiting." Knox shook his head in disbelief. "Norma and Edgar must have been really active in the community, because their doorbell didn't stop ringing. People were coming in and out of the house like it was a public place. I made it a point to stay close to Norma. I couldn't even tell you why, other than even I was uncomfortable with all of the attention she was receiving."

Knox had mentioned before that he didn't like to be enclosed in small places. It was in a cave that he'd stumbled across Ammeline, so it made sense that he wouldn't ever again allow himself to be in that type of enclosed environment.

And rightly so, dear hexed one. You are the same when it comes to public places. Look at where you're sitting, as opposed to my sweet Piper.

"I overheard Norma crying, saying that it had been her own hot chocolate that Edgar had taken from the side table," Knox explained, finally revealing the reason that Edgar might not have been the intended victim. "She'd set her drink down and gone back into the kitchen, believing that he'd wanted a cup of hot cider. He apparently drank half of it before getting up to see what was keeping her. Norma came through the doorway and—"

"She was standing underneath the mistletoe, and her husband kissed her," I whispered in dismay, finishing Knox's story for him. I'd seen everything in my premonition. "Edgar just fell to the floor after that. Poor Norma."

It was quite dreadful to watch. I'm sure it doesn't give her comfort, but the love we witnessed between them tells me that he would have willingly sacrificed himself for her, anyway.

I agreed with Pearl, but someone still had to be brought to justice for what they did to a loving couple. What was so wrong in today's world that someone would resort to murder?

We'd be here for another two thousand years if I were to start saying the list aloud, dear hexed one. It's our job to solve this case, and we will do exactly that. My sweet Piper, who does your app say is the prime suspect with this new information?

Chapter Nine

"WE DON'T HAVE enough information," Piper revealed, taking the last bite of her grilled cheese sandwich. She used her napkin to wipe her fingers. "Everything still points to Gracie Lynn as the prime suspect."

How so, my dear?

"Well, there are motives on this app," Piper explained, reaching for her glass of water. Pearl had already consumed her spot of lukewarm cream, and Knox had finished eating well before us. "It is basically saying that Gracie Lynn lost something in her life due to Edgar not being able to find a loophole in her lease, so she then took something from him in retaliation."

"Orwin has already ruled her out, so…"

Knox and Piper carried on the conversation while I checked the time on my phone. Orwin had texted that he was on his way back with Gracie Lynn. He didn't say much in his message other than Gracie Lynn definitely wasn't our murderer. It shouldn't be long before he joined us, which was why we'd ordered him something to eat. The BLT sandwich and fries had already been served and his plate was waiting for him.

It is a good thing I had a hearty breakfast, otherwise that spot of lukewarm cream and tuna sandwich wouldn't have been enough to get me through to dinner. It was a bit tepid. I have a feeling that waitress—the one who dislikes cats—didn't do as she was instructed. Are there any cards to leave our opinion on, dear hexed one? The owner should know about her lack of attention to details.

"I think it comes back to Debbie and Roger Wilkes," I said, having thought through the scenario ever since Knox dropped his bombshell. Apparently, Norma had told the detectives that it had been her drink, but they were still focused on Gracie Lynn due to her public threat. "Roger Wilkes was at the Booneville residence that day, and it's in writing that Debbie quit over not being made a partner in the business."

It stands to reason that those two detectives utilize my sweet Piper's app, too.

"Julie Kirkham did seem a bit rattled when we mentioned Debbie's name," Piper pointed out, quickly adding that detail to her notes. "Although, Vanessa said that wasn't why she quit, and we never did hear the real reason behind her resignation."

"It wasn't brought up in the car ride over to Mrs. Booneville's house, either." Knox reached for his wallet, though I did try to stop him. It was a long story, but the short end of it was that I had a trust fund. Granted, I'd spent three quarters of it on the RV so that we could have some type of base that could accommodate all of us. I was using the rest of the money to fund Operation Lich Queen. Knox always seemed to want to contribute to that fund. "We're partners, remember?"

I released Knox's arm with a simple nod after we had a brief staring contest, completely understanding his logic. We were partners, and we were in this together.

The waitress could have easily set my spot of cream down on the table between the two of you instead of shorting me seconds in the microwave. I'm sure my treat would have been either the perfect temperature or brought to a boiling point.

"I'll head back to the Booneville residence," Knox said, reaching for his winter coat that he'd hung on the back of the chair after sliding his wallet into the pocket of his jeans. "Once I get an answer on the Wilkes thing, I'll shoot you a text."

"Knox, what reason did you give Vanessa for why you were outside of her aunt and uncle's house?" Piper asked, her blue eyes looking up at him with curiosity.

Knox had all but indicated that Vanessa didn't know anything about his curse or what our true mission was with these murders. It did beg to question what excuse he'd given to the niece of the murder victim.

Beg? Did you just inadvertently express a dog pun, dear hexed one?

"I knew there was something I forgot to mention," Knox said, snapping his fingers as he flashed that charming smile of his. "We promised a friend that we'd check out Gracie Lynn's involvement, seeing as she's falsely presenting as one of us."

"And she fell for that?" Piper asked with disbelief, though she was truly the most trusting of our traveling band of mystery solvers. Pearl had pretty much expressed my thoughts, which had Piper glaring our way. "Fine. I might have believed that excuse myself, but that doesn't mean I wouldn't have eventually begun to wonder the validity of it."

"Which is why I should get back to the house." Knox buttoned his jacket and adjusted the shearling lapels. "I'll let Vanessa know that Gracie Lynn had nothing to do with her uncle's murder. See all of you back here for dinner at around five o'clock."

We all agreed to the time, but I couldn't help but wonder what excuse Knox would give that we were staying around town for a bit if we'd all but proven our case that Gracie Lynn didn't murder Edgar Booneville.

Oh, look. It's the alien hunter, and he brought with him the local fortune teller. She does look a bit worse for wear after being questioned for a couple of hours, doesn't she?

Knox passed Orwin, the two stopping briefly to speak with one another. Gracie Lynn remained by Orwin's side, her hair a bit frizzier than it was the last time I saw at the café this morning. Her gaze had landed on us, which meant that Orwin had told her something about the reason we were in town.

"You don't think…" Piper's voice trailed off as Knox

finally left and Orwin once again began to make his way to the back of the diner with Gracie Lynn in tow. Piper turned in her seat so that she was once again facing me. "He wouldn't have told her the truth about us, right?"

Our alien hunter might think outside of the box, but there is no one more fiercely protective of our kind than him. Just look at the lengths he's going to in order to locate those little green visitors.

"No," I replied without missing a beat, while agreeing with Pearl. "Not a chance, so we need to let him do the talking first."

"Hey," Orwin greeted us, his nose a bit red from the cold outdoors. He did a double take when he looked at me, but that was probably because my cheek still held a tint of rouge from the snowball. "I don't want to know, do I?"

I will tell you all the details over a proper spot of warm cream after we solve this murder mystery, alien hunter. It was quite entertaining.

"Actually," Piper began with a smile until I arched my brow. She laughed before greeting Gracie Lynn. "Hi, there. My name's Piper. This is Lou. We met earlier at the café."

"Here you go," Orwin said, pulling out a chair for Gracie Lynn so that she was sitting next to Piper. He took the seat that Knox had just vacated. "Can we get you some coffee, a soft drink, water? Are you hungry?"

"I'll take a cup of chamomile tea, please," Gracie Lynn responded after clearing her throat. "I need something to take the edge off, but I couldn't eat a thing after that horrible experience."

Clearly, my idea of taking the edge of with a glass or two of wine was completely different than Gracie Lynn's remedy.

Actually, I prefer the minty herb for those stressful times, though I try not to overindulge.

"I explained to Gracie Lynn that we're friends with Edgar Booneville's niece, but that we believe the police are looking in the wrong direction," Orwin said, having already shed his winter coat and rolled up the sleeves on his sweatshirt so that he could enjoy his lunch. Considering the running around he'd been doing, I was thinking we should have ordered him an extra side of fries. "She also knows that we're private investigators of sorts."

Private investigators? What was our alien hunter thinking with that cover story? Do we look like we live out of a...never mind. I'm rather impressed with Mr. Cornelia's quick thinking.

"I can't thank you enough for believing in my innocence," Gracie Lynn said with relief after Orwin had flagged down the waitress and placed her tea order. "I know there are some residents in this town who are skeptical of my abilities, but it's not right that they are fearful of my talent."

I haven't sharpened my claws recently, dear hexed one, and I'm certainly getting the itch to do so now.

Piper had a frown on her face that told me she was currently scolding her familiar for even having such thoughts. I couldn't reprimand Pearl when I had the same inclination to use my own ability to knock the woman out of her chair.

"You give people hope, Gracie Lynn," Orwin said in defense of the fortune teller, surprising all of us. "Your clients come to you for guidance, and you give it to them. Don't let anyone tell you differently."

Mr. Cornelia would like us to know that the local fortune teller is very cautious with her words, and that she actually uses a very specific train of chinwag to dole out information. Such as the flash sale at Go Out In Style. The boutique owner's mother is actually a regular client of Miss Hauver.

It made sense that Gracie Lynn would utilize the information she gleaned from her customers as a way of procuring people's beliefs in her fortunetelling abilities. Those bits of information gave her more credence and caused the doubters amongst the community to give her a wide berth.

"Why don't the two of you catch us up on what happened at the station," I suggested, lifting the glass of water the waitress had put on the table alongside my coffee. "The detectives obviously didn't have enough evidence to hold you."

"Detective Hadden was really focused on my argument with Edgar," Gracie Lynn replied, patting the frizz in her hair in a nervous gesture. I personally had never been on the receiving end of a police interrogation, but I wouldn't imagine the experience to be pleasant. "I explained over and over that I'd been upset about the contract, and even more so because Edgar wouldn't look for a loophole to keep me in a space I'd rented for the last three years. Edgar always found loopholes."

"Do you believe Mr. Booneville didn't want to find a loophole?" Piper inquired, asking the very same question that had popped into our minds.

"Let's just say that Norma isn't my number one fan," Gracie Lynn said wryly, dropping her hand into her lap. The clinking of her bracelets caught the attention of several patrons nearby. "I'm not sure Edgar even looked at my lease agreement."

"You should have someone else look at the terms of agreement then, especially since you only have two weeks left on your lease." I debated on whether or not to tell her that Roy had let himself into her shop, but he was the landlord. He had every reason to be inside, checking on things. My bet was that he'd been there to see if she was packing up her stuff. "Since you know that we're investigating Edgar's death, is there anything you can tell us that will help our investigation? Maybe you overheard someone say that he or she wanted to get back at the Boonevilles?"

Well worded, dear hexed one. Your inquiry includes Mrs. Booneville, whom we are now assuming was the intended victim.

"I only heard about Debbie Wilkes being upset that Norma didn't want to put their partnership in writing,"

Gracie Lynn said with a small shrug. Her tea was nowhere in sight. "I don't think Debbie or Roger would go so far as to actually murder someone. The Boonevilles and the Wilkes have been friends for years. Debbie went to work for Norma many years ago, and it wasn't until recently that Debbie wanted more of a stake in the knitting shop. After all, she'd been the one putting more hours in recently, allowing Norma to get things ready for Edgar's retirement. She was even planning a retirement party for him on New Year's Eve."

Very sad. Very sad, indeed.

"Do you have any customers who attend the bridge game on Thursday night?" Orwin asked, probably because he'd picked something up in Gracie Lynn's thoughts. A sneeze caught him off guard. "Did anyone else have a problem with the Boonevilles? Was anything mentioned in one of your sessions?"

"My sessions are private," Gracie Lynn said defensively, clearly offended that we would ask such a thing.

Yet the local fortuneteller utilizes the very same information to make others believe she is truly a psychic. Opposing morals, wouldn't you agree, dear hexed one?

I caught sight of the waitress carrying a tray that held Gracie Lynn's tea and discreetly held up a hand so that no one said something that could be spread around town. It was bad enough that Gracie Lynn thought we were private investigators, but anyone else believing that fabrication would have others cautious about their words.

We all fell quiet until the waitress had set the chamomile tea on the table. Once we answered her question regarding us needing anything more, she made her way over to an older couple who'd been arguing this entire time about how much money to spend on their grandchildren this holiday season.

Miss Hauver should check the temperature of her chamomile tea. We all know that the waitress tends to let things sit for too long.

Pearl was being a bit testy, which she happened to get when her spot of warm cream wasn't heated exactly to her desired temperature. I could see the steam rising out of Gracie Lynn's teacup.

Perfection. I can admit to being a tad bit envious.

"I do recall overhearing Edgar say something about his son-in-law on the morning we had our little disagreement." Gracie Lynn began to slowly dip the chamomile tea bag in and out of the hot water inside her cup as she allowed the anticipation to build. I could see how she could have someone eagerly awaiting news of his or her future. "Everyone but Abigail knew that Patrick was planning on surprising her by leasing an office here in town so that she could be closer to her parents. Edgar wasn't a fan of the young lawyer, if you catch my drift. He was very old school, which is why I thought he'd help me locate a loophole in my lease."

"Gracie Lynn, who was Edgar sitting with at the

diner the day the two of you had your argument?" I asked, setting down what was left of my water. It was always good to think outside the box in murder investigations, and I was all about expanding our suspect list. "Someone from town? Someone you knew?"

"Oh, yes!" Gracie Lynn exclaimed, making it seem that the individual was as nice as a warm piece of apple pie. "It was Roger Wilkes."

It is true that my tolerance for people such as Miss Hauver is rather on the thin side, but it's rare that I'd like nothing more than to hit my head against this wall behind us. My holiday cheer is getting snowed on between my spot of cream not being the right temperature and this local fortuneteller not seeing the significance of Mr. Booneville's guest at the diner. We'll need to remedy this rather quickly, dear hexed one.

Chapter Ten

"**Y**OU CAN'T EVISCERATE the local fortuneteller," Orwin complained, stepping outside and holding the door open so that Piper and I could follow closely behind. Gracie Lynn had already left the diner, saying that she had some clients this afternoon. "What is it with you and that word?"

It flows off my tongue quite nicely, don't you think? And what is so wrong with doing this small town a favor, alien hunter? It's very respectable to be kind to strangers. It's a way to invite good karma into your life.

"Good karma would be—"

"Let's put our opposing views aside for now," I interjected into Orwin and Pearl's banter. "We need to try and figure out how we can pay the Wilkes a visit without them getting suspicious of us."

There was an upbeat holiday carol coming out of the numerous speakers that had been positioned around their town square. Laughter from the children still having their snowball fight could be heard over the melody, as well as the wailing coming from the younger ones who were becoming impatient waiting in line to visit good ol' St. Nick. The patrons walking up and down the sidewalks seemed to have doubled since we'd eaten lunch.

I wonder if that waitress will be working the dinner shift. We really should find out before returning to a place we know doesn't put the care into their patrons' meals.

"I had to come up with a couple of opposing stories during my run-ins with the landlord and the realtor, so what we say from this point on could come back and bite us on the nose like Jack Frost snorting antifreeze," I muttered, stepping to the side to allow an elderly couple to enter the diner. I could only hope that Pearl hadn't retaliated in any way due to her spot of cream not being warmed properly. "Any ideas?"

Yes, and they all end in eviscerating a particular waitress. By the way, did you notice the way she chomped on that blue gum of hers? Chewing her gum like a cow chews its cud…just disgraceful.

"Why don't I head to the boutique with Piper," Orwin suggested, pushing up his glasses. He'd already put on his leather gloves after having used a tissue to wipe his nose. Being near Pearl all through lunch had wreaked havoc on his sinuses. "I'll get a quick read on the owner. That will give us time to figure out how to get near Debbie Wilkes."

"Sounds good," Piper said, adjusting her knitted scarf so that the biting wind couldn't reach her neck. "Lou, are you coming with us?"

I debated for a moment, but then decided to walk to an office we hadn't thought to check. It meant having to walk back through the winter wonderland and expose myself to what seemed to be a massive snowball fight that now included some of the parents, but it could be just the incentive we needed to solve this mystery.

I'm ready to solve this case and get back to our sanctuary. I've come to love our home on wheels, along with the microwave that heats beverages to perfection.

"You two go on ahead," I said, knowing that Pearl would stay with me if Orwin accompanied Piper. "I think I'll pay a visit to the Booneville Law Office. What was Edgar's administrative assistant's name?"

Edgar's hometown business had included him and a paralegal slash administrative assistant. He'd kept his clientele to locals, made a good living, and had never felt the need to expand. Technically, Roy had been his client, so it stood to reason that Edgar had written the very lease agreement that Gracie Lynn had signed. If she had been upset by the fine print, then maybe some of the other residents had hard feelings due to that exact reason.

The assistant's name was on one of the papers I'd left in the Jeep, but there had been so many people in connection to this murder. The voicemail on Edgar's business line had all but said that the office was permanently closed, and to contact another lawyer the next town over for any current cases. The two lawyers must have had an agreement in place for this eventuality.

Speaking of agreement, it's possible that the assistant was aware of the verbal pact between Mrs. Booneville and Mrs. Wilkes. Very well done, dear hexed one. This case is sledding right along now that you've had the proper nourishment…unlike me.

"Lynn Markle," Orwin replied, not bothering to wipe off the flurry that had landed on his right lens. It had melted immediately, leaving an itsy-bitsy pearl of water. "I doubt that she's there, but it's definitely worth a shot. Shoot us a text if you can get inside the office. We can meet you there."

"Will do." I slid my hands inside my pockets for warmth, still not willing to give in to the need for gloves. My ability to move things could be done through the leather, but I still loathed the feeling of my hands being smothered. "If you don't hear from me, meet me back at the knitting shop. I have a few follow-up questions for Julie regarding Debbie and Norma, and I'm hoping you can get a read on her. Julie definitely knows more than she's saying about Debbie's resignation."

You realize that by going back into the hobby shop, you are all but guaranteeing that we'll be wearing knitted hats, scarves, and mittens for the rest of the winter? That doesn't include the toaster cover, oven mitts, coffee coasters, and whatever else can be covered in the RV. My sweet Piper never does things halfway, dear colleagues.

Orwin and Piper began their walk down to the boutique shop while I navigated the small cobblestone path through the winter wonderland. I was keeping my fingers crossed that this new laid-out plan, plus Orwin's presence, could accelerate our progress on this murder mystery.

I have another idea that could potentially hasten our visit, though it does go against one of our top five rules.

"I'm all ears," I murmured, noticing that two of Santa's helpers were standing in line for a hot apple cider. Good ol' St. Nick must be on break from listening to the list of toys that the children had on their wish list this year. "Besides, it was Orwin who came up with those five rules."

And for very good reason, dear hexed one.

Two of the rules didn't even apply to Pearl. The binary policies regarding technology had more to do with Orwin's belief in alien life than they did our government—text in code if the message was something that shouldn't be intercepted and always have the location services off unless it was a life or death situation.

I'm going to try and not take offense to your lack of faith in my abilities, dear hexed one.

I managed to get through the winter wonderland without being an unintended target in the snowball fight that still ensued in earnest. Maybe there was a contest I didn't know about, though I didn't notice it on the town's holiday events calendar posted at the café. What had grabbed my attention was the wine tasting at the local liquor store tonight at seven o'clock. Now that was a festivity that I could wrap my mind around.

If I have my way, we won't be in Covered Bridge at

seven o'clock this evening. I'd rather be in our traveling home, enjoying a spot of warm cream that has been heated properly. It's only a little after noon, so we have many hours given in order to solve this mystery. Now, back to this idea of mine. Ms. Kirkham mentioned that the Wilkes lived on Passage Lane. Why don't I go pay them a quick visit to see if the couple might be discussing their dubious crime of murder?

It did appear that the Wilkes might have conspired to commit murder, or at least the wife had ample motive to kill Edgar, but it still seemed as if we were missing a big piece of the puzzle. I was hoping that Ms. Markle might be of help in that department. It did make sense for Pearl to pop in and out of the Wilkes' residence in an attempt to acquire a confession.

Pop in and out of the Wilkes' residence? Do I look like a weasel to you, Miss Lilura? And while we're on the subject of weasels, since when have you known me to enter a residence without a proper invitation? I will simply show up on their doorstep in my glorious, pristine form. Only a heartless criminal would be able to leave a lovely cat such as myself out in the cold. My own words give me pause.

"Why is that?" I asked now that we were away from the crowd.

We'd made it two blocks down, having already passed the café. I'd already checked on my Wrangler since we were on this end of town, and my baby was still sitting pretty.

That waitress was heartless. We should check to see if she had any motive to kill Mr. Booneville. He might very well have not had his oatmeal heated to the right temperature, and it is possible he complained on one of those cards you wouldn't allow me to fill out. She could have seen his complaint and decided to poison him with mistletoe.

"Who knew you had such an imagination on you, Pearl?" Maybe having a bit of distance between Pearl and the diner wasn't such a bad thing. "Go pay a visit to the Wilkes. Meet me back here as soon as you can."

Very well, but I am going to have my sweet Piper add that waitress to our suspect list. Remember, it's always whom we least expect.

I pondered that sentiment as I neared the law office of Edgar Booneville. Maybe that's why I was having such a hard time believing that Debbie and Roger Wilkes would murder Edgar. Norma would have been the obvious suspect, and directly behind her would have been Gracie Lynn. We were all pretty certain that neither one had poisoned Edgar, but what were the odds that the Wilkes would follow through with something so heinous with there being an email trail regarding their motive?

It was a surprise to find that the door to Edgar's business was open. Considering that the bell above rang the moment I pushed it open a crack, I didn't have much choice but to enter. I did so cautiously, not knowing exactly what I would find inside. To my relief, a woman in her sixties was sorting through files on a desk.

"Excuse me," I called out softly, not wanting to be the cause of anyone else dropping dead. "Are you Ms.

Markle?"

"Yes, I am," Lynn replied, studying me over the top of her reading glasses. "May I help you?"

Now was the time I needed to make a decision on how to handle this situation. Did I say that I was friends with Vanessa? If I went that route, there really would be no need for me to stop by this office. If I went with the journalist spin, it was highly doubtful that Lynn would talk to me. I couldn't tell her the truth, either. She'd all but kick me to the curb.

"My name is Lou, and I was hoping you could help me look over a lease I'm about to sign." I somehow managed not to cringe at the direction I'd taken, not knowing why this case had me all but sideways with my various cover stories. Usually, I picked one and stuck to it. We were less likely to get caught in a lie. Yet here I was, all but holding up a sign and saying I was a liar. "Susan mentioned you by name."

"Susan?" Lynn frowned, taking off her glasses as she motioned for me to come closer. "I'm not sure why she would say such a thing. The lawyer who owned this office recently passed away. We're actually closed, and I was going through active cases to give to Doug Pinkston in Fargo. I can give you his number, if you like."

"Susan actually told me about Mr. Booneville," I confessed, trying my best to appear innocuous. Piper was the one who had the ability to appear innocent, mostly because she was so trustworthy. I'd gotten over that the moment I had my encounter with Ammeline. "I'm sorry for your loss. I almost didn't even stop by the office, believing you'd be closed."

"Well, it was just me and Edgar." Lynn set down her glasses on top of the files before pushing back her chair. She gave me a sad smile as she picked up her mug and made her way around the desk. "Coming into the office keeps me busy, and these files won't transfer themselves. Did Susan give you the indication that Edgar had a partner?"

"No, not at all," I said truthfully while trying to figure out a way to keep talking about Edgar. "I figured since you worked so long with Mr. Booneville that maybe you'd know a little of the verbiage on the local leases. I have it here in my email, if you could just take a quick peek at it."

I made the pretense of pulling out my phone and scrolling through my email while Lynn poured herself another cup of coffee. What I was actually doing was texting Orwin and letting him know that Lynn was working today, and that I would keep her occupied until he and Piper could head this way.

A strange sensation washed over me, but I chalked it up to not having Pearl here to commentate every now and then. Either that or it was the fact that I caught Lynn watching me in the mirror above the small coffee station.

"I did help Edgar draft up the paperwork, but I'm

really not a lawyer," Lynn said cautiously after noticing that I'd caught her watching me. "You're not from here, are you?"

Lynn Markle had probably been born and raised in Covered Bridge, so she knew very well that I wasn't from these parts. Mentioning Susan's name had worked for a brief moment to get my foot in the door. Now that Lynn had time to think about, though, she was probably realizing that Susan wouldn't have revealed so much to an outsider.

"No, but I'm in love with this town," I responded, still keeping up pretenses that I was searching for the lease in my email. I scrunched my nose and met Lynn's gaze as she strolled toward me. "I'll admit to being hesitant about opening a shop up in this town, though. I saw the police escort a woman into the back of a police car this morning."

I lowered my phone, knowing full well that I'd caught Lynn's attention. Gossip had a tendency to do that in a small town such as Covered Bridge. Right about now was when Pearl would have told me I'd make a great fisherman. She sure was taking her time over at the Wilkes. I bet they gave her a spot of warm cream.

"That's just Gracie Lynn," Lynn scoffed as she made her way back around her desk. She sat down and wheeled herself close enough so that her elbows rested on the hard surface, maintaining a hold on her coffee. She even blew lightly over the rim in an attempt to cool the coffee. "I wouldn't worry too much about her. She's always getting herself into those types of scrapes. If you talked to Susan, then I'm sure you heard all about Gracie Lynn being a suspect in Edgar's murder. I'm here to tell you that the woman wouldn't hurt a fly. Do you know that she stopped traffic on the onramp in order to save Mrs. Lewis' toy poodle? Gracie Lynn is just a bit odd, is all. She's actually a very nice person."

Lynn took a tentative sip of her coffee, testing the temperature.

"Edgar was a good man," Lynn said with a sad smile after setting her coffee cup in between the numerous stacks of files. "He was also a good lawyer, and his contracts were concrete. There was nothing that Gracie Lynn could have done to extend her lease. Besides, I heard through the grapevine that someone wants to open up a printing shop. You know, the ones that do t-shirts, mugs, and such."

"If Mr. Booneville was such a good man, who would want to kill him?"

I wanted to keep the momentum of the conversation flowing now that Lynn didn't seem so suspicious of my motives anymore. Orwin and Piper couldn't get here soon enough. He'd be able to get close enough to Lynn to hopefully gain any insight or doubt that might exist about her boss.

"No one," Lynn replied with what appeared to be true bewilderment and utter sadness. She reached for her reading glasses, but didn't put them on. A lot of people needed to keep busy when faced with a tragedy such as this. It was no wonder she had the need to come into the office and get his business affairs in order. She most likely felt she was contributing in some way. "Edgar was loved by everyone, and Gracie Lynn was just upset when she confronted him at the diner. No one had any reason to kill him. Honestly, stuff like this doesn't happen here. There are rumors that he ingested the poison by mistake, and I'm inclined to agree with that theory."

"What about his wife?" I asked, following up that question with a bit of insight that wouldn't have Lynn mistrustful of my intentions. "I watch a lot of those crime shows on television, and they always have a twist where the victim wasn't the intended victim."

"Norma? Well, she could be a shrewd businesswoman, that's for sure," Lynn replied, but she was shaking her head while she did so. "But again, nothing happens like that in Covered Bridge. I think I know the show you're talking about, though. 'NCIS', right? No, no. I think it might have been on 'Bones' or 'Castle'. Oh, I do miss those two shows."

Confession time. I travelled in an RV to save people from being victims of murder. I didn't have time to watch television, though I did catch snippets from when Piper was curled up on the couch and streaming the shows on her laptop. In my defense, I had heard of those television shows, only I hadn't known that two of them were now off the air.

The only thing that stood out was the shrewd comment regarding Norma. We'd already established it was more than likely she had been the intended victim, so maybe it did come full circle to the Wilkes.

"Here, dear." Lynn slipped on her reading glasses and flipped through an old Rolodex. I didn't even think those were made anymore. Within seconds, she was holding out a business card for me to take. "This is Doug Pinkston's card. Call the number listed, and I'm sure that he'll be able to review that lease agreement."

"I appreciate it," I replied, wondering what was keeping Orwin and Piper. I really couldn't force the conversation more than I already had, but I truly didn't think Lynn knew anything more that could help with the case. It was best I leave so that Lynn wasn't calling Susan the moment I walked out the door. "Again, I'm sorry for your loss."

If the Wilkes are guilty, I'll eat that aluminum hat of Mr. Cornelia's!

I wasn't the accident-prone type, but Pearl's sudden entrance had me hitting the doorframe on my way out. I lifted my hand to let Lynn know that I was okay, thinking maybe she said to have a happy holiday, but the vibrations of the old oak door were still ringing in my ears.

"I swear, I'm going to get a bell to go around your neck," I muttered after I'd closed the door behind me.

Flurries were still floating down from the overcast sky, but the bitter wind seemed to have thankfully died down a bit. "Did Mrs. Wilkes give you a spot of warm cream?"

Yes, indeed! They are the nicest couple, dear hexed one. Of course, it took me a while to show them what I wanted. They were quick learners, those two.

"Just because they gave you a spot of warm cream heated to perfection does not mean they are not killers," I commented wryly, wondering what happened to the wise familiar from this morning. "You're not turning into Piper on me, are you?"

Don't be silly, Miss Lilura. I have a very good nose for the guilty, and Mr. and Mrs. Wilkes are not among them. I did so happen to get a look at Mr. Wilkes' email that he had up on his laptop.

I shoved Doug Pinkston's business card in my coat pocket. I'd been scanning the sidewalk for any sign of Orwin and Piper when Pearl's words had registered in my mind. She'd found something.

Yes, I did. I'm quite proud of my detective skills, too.

Someone was walking our way, and I didn't want to appear as if I'd lost one my marbles that Pearl was always saying had rolled off, so I purposefully smiled and nodded my head as we passed one another. I did my best to remain patient, but it wasn't easy when the answers to this murder mystery were within reach.

I won't make you wait, dear hexed one. You'll be happy to know that Mr. Booneville had sent an email to Mr. Wilkes expressing his sincere apologies for what appears to have been a misunderstanding. The message was dated the day before Mr. Booneville's death, and in it were arrangements for the two couples to have lunch this week. The Wilkes had no motive, Miss Lilura. None whatsoever, so it looks as if we're back to square one—with no suspect!

Chapter Eleven

"**H**AVING NO SUSPECTS does pose a problem."

I continued to walk down the sidewalk, mindful of any slick spots. The festivities in town square were still going strong, and it also appeared as if some of the family events had begun. Behind where Santa Claus' extravagant chair had been positioned was a small manmade hill no taller than six feet that had been packed with snow. Eager young children holding small rubber tubes were lined up in a single file.

I suggest sending a message to Mr. Emeric in hopes that he can ask Mrs. Booneville exactly what happened to cause such a misunderstanding.

"My thoughts exactly," I said, already having my phone in hand so that I could find out where Orwin and Piper had gotten to after they'd visited the boutique. "Orwin also needs to see if somehow the police have come up with anything new in regard to fingerprints on the mug that they bagged as evidence."

That uncomfortable sensation I'd experienced when talking with Lynn came over me once again, causing me to step to the side so that I wasn't in anyone's way. It almost felt like nausea, but it was highly doubtful there had been anything wrong with my bowl of soup.

Unless those bits of chicken were bad, dear hexed one. I certainly wouldn't put anything past that waitress. I wouldn't be surprised if she'd been the one to leave the chicken out too long before the cook made the pot of fresh soup this morning.

The thought of food poisoning made my stomach lurch once more. The cold air helped a bit, and I even managed to shoot off a text to Knox, Orwin, and Piper. I included all three in the group message so that we were all on the same page.

Don't forget to tell them about my visit to the Wilkes. Such a lovely couple.

Piper replied immediately, though that wasn't uncommon. Apparently, they were still at the boutique, chatting away with the owner.

A Chatty Cathy. My sweet Piper and the alien hunter could be there a while. We should start to head that way, Miss Lilura. Maybe Chatty Cathy can give us a new lead. At this rate, we won't be solving this murder mystery anytime soon.

I had already begun heading that way, needing to cross the street. The fastest way was on the path where I'd been hit in the face with a snowball, but the battle seemed to have tapered off. My phone notified me that I'd received another message. A quick peek showed that Knox agreed to sneak a moment with Norma in hope to find out more about this misunderstanding.

I'm sure that Norma has access to Mr. Booneville's email. Perhaps Miss Carlisle could ask to use one of their computers. One would assume that two business owners would have a couple of desktops, along with laptops.

Pearl had a good idea, though I wasn't sure just how many of those computers the police would have taken as evidence. Either way, it was worth a shot. I'd made it halfway through the winter wonderland when a wave of nausea hit me so hard in the stomach that my knees almost crumbled.

Oh, dear!

Pearl's sentiment was well warranted, and I now realized what was wrong.

This is not good. Not good at all.

"This is out and out bad, Pearl," I murmured, hoping beyond hope that my knees didn't buckle.

There's a bench to your left, Miss Lilura. Sit. Sit right this minute, and I'll be back in a jiffy.

Pearl was never one to panic or lose her sense of composure during an emergency, but this wasn't the typical situation where we got caught snooping for information. No, this was much worse. This was the direst of cataclysms. You see, only one reason could be at fault for such a violent reaction.

Ammeline Letty Romilda was within one hundred miles of our location.

Pearl was right about the seat. I really needed to sit down. I carefully made my way to the bench that Pearl had pointed out before she'd gone to find Orwin and Piper. Orwin had helped me cast a proximity spell within days of my hex, but this was the first time since then that I'd ever felt the side effects. I'm not even sure how I recognized the severe nausea as a sign of the Lich Queen's presence, but I was one hundred percent confident in my deduction. As a matter of fact, Pearl had recognized the sign, as well.

"Are you alright, miss?"

By the time I'd evened out my breathing and gotten my physical response under control, I'd made it to the bench. I hadn't even realized that someone else had been sitting on the opposite side, let alone that it was a large man in a red suit. His cheeks and nose were rosy, and his blue eyes contained concern for my welfare. Leave it to me to sit next to Santa Claus while one of the vilest creatures on the face of the planet was hunting me.

Technically, I didn't know if Ammeline was hunting me. She could simply be in North Dakota for the scenery this holiday season. I did my best not to let out a hysterical laugh that would have good ol' St. Nick heading for his sleigh.

"I'm fine, Santa," I replied with a half-smile. I raised my face to the flurries floating down from the sky, grateful for their refreshing coolness. For once today, I didn't mind being outside in the cold. "Let's just say I just received some unsettling news."

"Unsettling?" Santa nodded his head, as if I'd just

told him the secret to flying that sleigh he was no doubt wishing he was on at the moment. "I like you. You have a good outlook, dear."

"I'll need you to say that again when my friends are here," I replied lightheartedly, the tension slowly easing out of my body. Don't get me wrong. Ammeline was still within the hundred-mile radius, but my body was becoming accustomed to the warning signs of the spell. "I'm definitely not known for my optimism."

Now that I had somewhat of a handle on my composure, I thought through our options. Would the effects of the proximity spell become stronger the closer we became or was this it? We could begin our search for her, relying on Knox to use his senses to seek her out. He had her scent locked in, so it shouldn't be too hard to find her location.

"Maybe it's the Christmas spirit." Santa took a bite out of a cookie that he held in a napkin, chewing on it while he contemplated the possibility of…a Christmas miracle? Maybe. I'm sure Pearl would have agreed, but I'd lost all faith in miracles the day I'd had my run-in with Ammeline. "We do tend to look at things differently this time of year. My job is quite hard, you know. There's a trick to granting wishes and giving gifts to those in need."

"A trick?" I asked, wishing I hadn't. This Santa Claus was just a representation of the Christmas holiday, and nothing more. Besides, I had places to be and a Lich to see, all starting with one of the plans put in place by my team. We'd gone over many scenarios, and now we had to choose one wisely. I didn't need to be rude, though. "Aren't you one of the many helpers to the real Santa Claus, gathering the wish lists of all the little boys and girls?"

I knew firsthand that we didn't always know who was around to overhear us. With all the children running around this amazing winter wonderland, I didn't want to take away their hope that Santa had the ability to be in multiple places all at once.

"Tommy Little wants a new bike for Christmas, but I know that his older sister is saving up her allowance to buy it for him for his birthday," Santa Claus confided in me after he'd taken another bite of his cookie. His blue eyes were no longer deepened with concern, but instead they were sparkling with joy. "Unfortunately, Tommy's birthday isn't until February."

"So, you're saying the trick is somehow trying to figure out how to relay that information to Tommy's parents," I guessed, not sure why I was still having this conversation. There was something about the man's tone that suggested deep wisdom. Maybe something inside of me yearned to be told how to handle an extremely complicated situation, even though there was nothing anyone could say to make the upcoming confrontation any less difficult. "I can understand your situation, Santa. Being privy to information when others aren't can be a heavy weight. It makes for many sleepless nights."

I wasn't sure how Tommy's bike situation could cause Santa sleepless nights. I mean, he really only needed to tell the boy's parents. Didn't it make sense that Mr. and Mrs. Little could help the sister reach her goal, thereby allowing Tommy to receive his gift on Christmas morning?

"I have many sleepless nights, Miss Lilura," Santa said as he gestured toward all the children laughing and screaming in delight as they each had their turn sledding down the miniature hill. "I have a lot of miracles to fulfill."

"Miracles?" I didn't want to make light of what this man did during the season, but there were no miracles to be given in his position. I guess I could see where he would have sleepless nights not being able to fulfill the wishes of those children, though. "I haven't seen a miracle in some time, Santa."

"I disagree. We're given a miracle every single day, my dear," Santa Claus replied after he'd taken another bite of his sugar cookie. "Aren't we provided a miracle every morning with a fresh start? It's how we use the new beginning that rests on us."

The only fresh thing I'd been looking at this morning was this murder mystery, and now I would have to postpone giving Mrs. Booneville closure. I wasn't one to put things off, but this investigation would definitely have to be put on hold seeing as we were so close to our goal. On second thought, maybe this was a Christmas miracle.

I daresay I've arrived just in time to ensure that you haven't let all of your marbles escape that head of yours. What is this talk of miracles?

"Ho-ho-ho!" Santa exclaimed in jolliness, causing me to startle a bit. He even rested his hand on his belly as he finished his ho-ho-hoing with a chuckle. I wasn't sure what he found so entertaining. "Just remember, Miss Lilura, all miracles come in different ways. You'll see. You just need a bit of patience."

Once again, I leave you for mere minutes only to find you in quite the conundrum with St. Nicholas. Since when do you believe in miracles, dear hexed one?

"I see your friends are here to make sure that you're feeling alright," Santa said in approval, crumbling his napkin in his white glove as he used the armrest of the bench to help him stand. "Perhaps you shall receive your gift from me early this year, Miss Lilura. I do believe you need a bit of faith. Now, I'm off to see about that Tommy Little issue. Merry Christmas to the both of you."

I'd been looking up as Orwin and Piper frantically crossed the street to reach the cobblestone path when what good ol' St. Nick said hit me harder than the nausea had a few minutes ago. I had to have heard the man wrong, but there was no sign of him anywhere. Seriously, he had just vanished into thin air.

Impossible, dear hexed one. I'm not sure what just took

place, but I will get to the bottom of it. He couldn't have gotten far.

"The proximity spell worked?" Orwin asked in astonishment, a bit out of breath. His face was flushed, but I wasn't so sure that was due to the cold. "I can't believe it. We need to call Knox and—"

"Did you see which way Santa Claus went?" I didn't mean to cut Orwin off, but I needed to find St. Nick.

I've gone to all four sides of this town square, and I can't find hide nor beard of him, dear hexed one. Are you thinking what I'm thinking?

"Santa Claus?" Piper asked, sharing a worried glance with Orwin. "Why? What does Santa Claus have to do with Ammeline? And Pearl, Santa is in his big chair in the middle of the park. There was no need to hit each corner of town square. I already texted Knox, and he said that he'll…"

Piper continued to talk about how Knox would meet us back at the RV, but all I could focus on was Santa Claus…only he wasn't the right one.

I think it's time we consider the alternative, dear hexed one.

"Don't say it. That's impossible," I muttered, causing Orwin and Piper once again to exchange worrying glances. I'd turned around in three complete circles, hoping to catch sight of the man I'd just spent a few minutes talking to while sitting on the bench. "He's got to be here somewhere."

In case you didn't hear him, he knew your name. He

also spoke to the both of us. That would mean he knew of my existence while in my unseen form. I do believe there could be a slim chance that we might have actually met—

"A warlock," I stated very matter-of-factly, not willing to believe anything else. "Maybe Ammeline sent a warlock here to see what we were up to?"

"Okay, that's enough," Piper announced, holding up her mittens so that Pearl and I would stop guessing as to the appearance of the man in the red suit. "You two are now just throwing out theories without any evidence."

"There's probably an app on your phone that tries to figure out if—"

"I didn't imagine an entire conversation about miracles with a man in a red suit on this very bench," I insisted to both Orwin and Piper, both of whom were assuming the proximity spell had me taking leave of my senses. "Pearl, tell them."

That wise jolly man did make a very compelling case that had us believing he could indeed be the one and only Santa Claus. I suppose in retrospect St. Nicholas is magical, so it stands to reason that he would be able to know of my presence.

"Wait a second," Orwin said, stepping closer so that a family who was walking by couldn't eavesdrop. "Could you hear him, cotton ball?"

Pearl hated when Orwin called her by that nickname, but it had become rather second nature to him. I didn't want to stand here to hear another argument ensue when a warlock working for Ammeline could very well be making his escape.

The alien hunter has a point, dear hexed one. I don't believe so, especially since all I could hear was that annoying reindeer song. I would have sworn on my favorite brand of cream that the lyrics only last a minute or two.

"Song?" I asked, finally relenting that the Santa who had been sitting next to me on the bench was no longer in the area. "The song coming out of the speakers was 'Santa Claus is Coming to Town'."

No, dear hexed one. I'm positive it was the reindeer song, because I recall thinking I'd like to take that red nose and—

"You're not eviscerating Rudolph, cotton ball," Orwin muttered, preventing Pearl from incriminating herself should anything happen to one of the deer in the petting zoo that was coming to town tomorrow. I really, really didn't want to have to come back here after hunting down Ammeline. "Piper and I could hear the song coming out of the speakers clearly, and Lou is right about which song was playing."

What are you trying to say, alien hunter? If you so much as suggest that my two thousand years on this earth could lend itself to dementia, it's not a red-nosed reindeer that I'll be eviscerating.

"Would you two just stop?" Piper whispered urgently, stepping close so that the three of us appeared to be having a private conversation. "This is serious. Lou believes that Ammeline might have sent a warlock to see what we were up to, all the while being within a hundred miles of our location. We all know that the infamous Lich Queen is off her rocker. There's no telling what she's up to, and we shouldn't be standing around as targets."

Piper was right, and I instinctively wanted to head to the Jeep so that we could seek safety in the RV until we decided which plan to utilize in our confrontation with Ammeline. I was leaning toward destroying her cane, particularly the crystal on the end. It was the phylactery that held her power, after all. If we managed to get rid of that, her soul could go to wherever it belonged.

"What I'm trying to say is that Pearl heard what St. Nick wanted her to hear," Orwin stressed, not letting any of us go anywhere. Where the cold air had been rather soothing when my nausea had been in full force, it was having the opposite affect now. I rubbed my hands together, unable to stop my gaze from attempting to seek out the warlock who could potentially be working with Ammeline. "Lou, he planted that song in your head so that you couldn't hear his thoughts. Knox did something similar to me when he first began crossing our paths."

I suppose the song did sound a bit odd, almost hollow. As a matter of fact, it was as if it was coming out of a Victrola. I'm a bit confused, alien hunter. Are you suggesting that we spoke with a warlock working with that despicable supernatural being or…

"What's going on?" Knox had come jogging up the cobblestone path, not one bit out of breath. His skin appeared sun-kissed, even in the middle of winter, and there wasn't even a hint of redness in his cheeks. His golden gaze landed on me, looking me up and down as if to make sure that I was okay. I honestly didn't know. "Lou? Piper said there'd been an emergency and to meet back at the RV, but I saw your Jeep still parked across from the café. Are you alright?"

You would do well to remember that your Mr. Emeric is a werewolf, dear hexed one. It is in his nature to hunt, and you're about to serve up his prey on a silver platter.

I understood and even agreed with Pearl to an extent, but this wasn't just my fight.

"Ammeline is within one hundred miles of us, Knox," I stated without hesitation. After all, we were in this together. "She's here."

This is the moment when St. Nicholas would ho-ho-ho.

Chapter Twelve

"**D**RINK UP," KNOX ordered, holding a cup of hot apple cider in front of me. Instead of driving away from this small town, we were now at the same table inside the bakery as we were this morning. "It will take the shivers away."

I'd begun shivering the longer we'd stood outside, but it hadn't been due to the weather. You see, the nausea that had overwhelmed me had simply vanished the moment I'd pulled the keys from my coat pocket. I'd been all set to hunt with Knox. Not in the literal sense, but I'd been ready to finally have a lead that could guide us to Ammeline.

Now?

It was gone, along with our chance to get our lives back.

You're about to go into one of your sulking moods, dear hexed one. You'll bring up miracles, how they don't exist, and then I'll be forced to come up with some spectacular knock-knock joke. Well, I simply won't allow it. Drink up, buttercup. We have a murder mystery to solve.

"Cotton ball is right," Orwin said quietly, wrapping his hands around his own hot apple cider. "We'll drive ourselves crazy with the whole what-if thing. I have thought of something, though."

It better be good or else that will be the last time you call me that, alien hunter.

"What's that, Orwin?" Piper asked, having taken the seat across from me.

No one had bothered to take off their jackets. This break was only going to last long enough for me to regain my composure. Truthfully, I was just angry more than anything. We'd had her, and then she'd simply vanished.

Had Ammeline somehow known our intentions?

Had she figured out that she was no longer the hunter?

On the other hand, Ammeline might simply have skirted past the radius of my proximity spell, on her way to a warmer area for her frail being. The bottom line was that we'd missed our chance, and the wasted opportunity was soul-crushing.

Let me dust off my knock-knock joke book, Miss Lilura. And here I thought we were going for a three-day streak.

I inhaled deeply, understanding why Pearl was pushing me to take a step forward instead of a step back. That didn't mean I had to like it.

"Well, we were only able to do the proximity spell based on Lou's curse," Orwin explained, pushing up his glasses before resting his elbows on the table. "Basically, any type of incantation such as that requires something from the caster. It's similar to a location spell."

"I never did understand why you couldn't simply do one of the scry things you do," Knox said, having opted for black coffee. He, too, was resting his elbow on the table as he got a better handle on what could and couldn't be done with magic. "Can't you use our curses for a locator spell if you were able to use it for the other one?"

"In normal circumstances, yes," Orwin replied. "But we're dealing with a witch whose physical being has basically ceased to exist. A locator spell can only locate physical items that have substance."

"A proximity spell works differently," Piper chimed in, studying Orwin as if she realized where he was going with his idea. No doubt, it would be brilliant. He was an amazing warlock, but it was his ability with technology that was bar none. "Ammeline is here for a reason. You're going to create one of those algorithm programs, aren't you?"

Fine, alien hunter. You've proved your worth. I won't put you on my evisceration list quite yet.

Piper admonished Pearl while Orwin just flashed a smile, almost as if he took her banter as a compliment.

"We've already done our research on Liches. They bind their intellect and what is left of their souls to a physical object," Orwin said, although he held up a hand when Knox was clearly confused about the material item. "We don't have anything from her cane to be able to use in a locator spell. But think about this—Liches like to hole up in one place, such as in a cave on a remote mountaintop where no one can find them. Ammeline has been to Washington and North Dakota, that we know of in less than a year. Why?"

"You're going to use the proximity spell to begin tracking Ammeline's visits." It was the first time I'd addressed our predicament since we sat down. Orwin's idea had merit, but it also required a load of patience. "Do you think she's looking for something?"

Or maybe someone, Pearl surmised. *You might be onto something, alien hunter. I'll reach out to some fellow familiars to see if they've heard any rumblings about the Lich Queen on a quest of her own.*

"If that's the theory we're going with, then who was the warlock in the Santa Claus suit?" I asked, not willing to let that slide. "He knew my name, as well as sensed Pearl's presence. We're gambling a lot if we let this slide."

In my two thousand years on this earth, dear hexed one, I have heard such rumors giving credence to a genuine St. Nicholas. What makes you so certain that he does not exist?

Piper quickly got Knox caught up on Pearl's side of the conversation. His tell of rubbing his five o'clock shadow was a sign of his own disbelief.

"It's not like we can do anything about it now," Orwin pointed out. "Your Santa is long gone, Lou."

We all sat in silence for a moment, begrudgingly accepting that our moment had come and gone. I took another sip of my hot apple cider, allowing the warmth of the beverage to spread through me as I thought back to my conversation with the warlock.

Santa Claus, dear hexed one.

"We could just call him Nick," Orwin said, joining in on the name game.

"Kris Kringle would work," Piper added, flashing me a smile.

"I need to start carrying around aspirin the way Orwin lugs around all those antihistamines," Knox muttered, running a hand down his face in lighthearted frustration. "Are we really trying to come up with a name for Father Christmas?"

"That was a good one," Orwin surmised, shooting me a glance to see if their merry discussion had lifted my spirits. I hated that they all felt the need to soothe my anxiety. "Why? Isn't that what friends are for?"

"Friends know when to give someone a bit of privacy, as well," I said with a pointed look. I did crack a smile, though. "I'm fine. Really. If Knox can handle the fact that he didn't get to go on the hunt of a lifetime today, then so can I."

"We'll find Ammeline," Knox promised, his already rich voice dropping another level. "You have my word."

Well, now, it's getting a tad bit warm in here, isn't it?

"We'll finish up here, and then we can head back to

the RV so that Orwin can start working on that algorithm," I said, putting a plan in place while ignoring Pearl's taunt about my friendship with Knox. Besides, I needed something to keep my mind off the fact that I wasn't going to be hex free by tonight. "Knox, were you able to speak with Norma about the email exchange between Edgar and Mr. Wilkes?"

"Sort of," Knox hedged, tilting his head in a so-so kind of manner. "Vanessa somehow managed to convince Norma that she needed access to Edgar's email. I read the exchange, but it was rather vague. It was almost as if they'd had a conversation beforehand about the pertinent facts of some misunderstanding, and this email was just a reminder that a lunch had been scheduled between the two couples. Oh, and there was mention of confusion over a date, but it was going to be a topic of their upcoming conversation."

"Maybe a future date on when Mrs. Booneville would make Mrs. Wilkes a full-time partner?" Piper mused, throwing out a theory as she gestured toward her phone she'd set on the table. "This app is worthless without all the facts. It really does make it hard not to be on the inside of an investigation."

Upon visiting the Wilkes, who are just lovely people, I did notice that there was a pumpkin pie in the oven. Perhaps it was made to take to Mrs. Booneville.

"That would suggest that the women had already made up, so maybe that's why the police don't feel as if the couple are viable suspects," Piper said, looking at Orwin for confirmation. "Unless the pumpkin pie was her way of apologizing."

"Maybe," Orwin answered, though he didn't look convinced. "The two detectives were pretty focused on Gracie Lynn, but we already know that she's innocent. It's sounding like the Wilkes aren't viable suspects, either. We're not left with a whole lot."

Knox leaned a little to his right as he reached inside the pocket of his winter coat. He pulled out his phone, looking down at the display. His frown was evident as he continued reading whatever message he'd just received.

Would you please prompt the wolfman to share, dear hexed one? We don't have all day.

Piper and I shared a look of amusement, because neither one of us were that foolish.

What namby-pambys. Mr. Cornelius, do you have a backbone?

"Oh, so now you use my proper name." Orwin made known that he was going to milk this moment. "You do realize that—"

Whatever Orwin was going to say to Pearl was cut off when Knox finally revealed why he was mystified by the message. Knox even pushed back his chair, indicating that it was time to leave.

"Vanessa said that the police confiscated Norma's laptop the other day, so she wants us to meet her at the knitting shop. She can access the email exchange between

Debbie and Norma on the shop's computer."

"We've already read them," Orwin pointed out with a frown of his own, which only caused him to sneeze. Technically, that was Pearl's fault. "Remember, I hacked into the knitting shop's mainframe. There wasn't anything in there other than Norma responding to Debbie's email to say that she wasn't ready to make her partner. Debbie's response was her resignation. Pretty cut and dried."

"Vanessa is already parked a few blocks down," Knox revealed, standing with his coffee cup in hand. "It's not like we have anything else to go on, so let's go meet her."

You realize that taking Piper back into that knitting shop is like taking a book addict into a bookstore, right?

"You can always steal her credit card," I suggested after everyone had begun walking toward the door. Quite honestly, today had felt like a wasted twenty-four hours. We'd run nonstop in what seemed like circles since this morning, and we were no closer to finding Edgar's killer than we were of locating Ammeline. On top of that, a knitting fanatic had been born. "I told you that you should have taught her to love crossword puzzles, Pearl. It's entirely your fault if I end up with knitted underwear."

That would certainly be a sight to see, dear hexed one. I do believe it's time to dust off my stealth skills.

Chapter Thirteen

"**H**EY," VANESSA GREETED Knox with a smile, even going so far as to toss her long brown hair over her shoulder. "Thanks for meeting me here."

Such a nice she-wolf, isn't she?

I didn't bother to reply, because I knew very well that Pearl was just trying to goad me into admitting that I'd been paid a visit by a little green monster. My visit with good ol' Kris Kringle had been more than enough for today.

"What is it that you think you'll find?" Knox asked, holding the door open for all of us as we filed into the knitting shop one by one. "Could you not access your aunt's email from her phone?"

"Well, Debbie stopped by with a pumpkin pie," Vanessa informed us, taking a moment to wave toward Julie, who was with a customer. "She mentioned that maybe after Uncle Edgar's funeral, they could sit down and talk about *the email*."

Vanessa had stressed the two words, as if Debbie had done the same.

Mrs. Wilkes is such a lovely lady, and her manners are impeccable, are they not?

"I read through their email exchange, Lou," Orwin stressed with a shake of his head. He'd had to remove his glasses after the lenses fogged up after entering the heated store so that he could clean them. "I don't get it."

"Well, let's find out before Piper buys any more patterns," I said, noticing that Piper had managed to collect two more books with multiple patterns in each. Visions of all of us in matching Christmas outfits from head to toe for the next ten years floated through my mind. "Oh, we're in so much trouble, aren't we?"

That crossbody purse of hers makes it very hard to gain access to her credit card, dear hexed one. Perhaps you could use your magic to break the credit card machine. No purchase means no more pattern books.

"Vanessa, dear, how is your aunt doing?" Julie asked, having disengaged with the customer long enough to greet us from across the shop. "I spoke with her first thing this morning, but the store has been so busy since then that I haven't had a chance to talk with her."

"A lot of the bridge club showed up today," Vanessa said, taking her gloves off as the heat in the shop become rather stifling. "Don't worry, though. They're following the meal schedule, but they brought in some smaller things for Aunt Norma to munch on here and there. Listen, Aunt Norma needed me to get some things from the office. Do you mind if I go into the back room?"

"Sure, go ahead," Julie replied, frowning when she

realized that we were with Vanessa. "Weren't you two in here earlier?"

It seems as if our cover story is about to be blown, dear hexed one. Now would be a good time to come up with a Plan B.

"Yes, we were," Piper replied with a sad smile. "I couldn't believe it when I found out that Vanessa was the niece of Mrs. Booneville. We went to summer camp together many times during our childhood. We ran into each other at the bakery, so we thought we'd tag along to keep her company. Do you have a moment? I'd love to talk about this scarf pattern while Vanessa does what she needs to do."

"Of course." Julie looked over her shoulder at the other customers before glancing uncomfortably at Knox. He could be a bit imposing with his military vibe. "Give me one moment to speak with Mrs. Barnett about her great-granddaughter's baby blanket."

My sweet Piper is so cunning to keep Ms. Kirkham busy while we basically invade a widow's privacy.

That was certainly a new opinion of our situation, but Pearl's obsession with etiquette had been tweaked a bit since we'd entered someone else's domain without their knowledge. Well, it was too late to go back. Plus, there were things we needed to do in order to get the end result. In this case—justice.

Piper motioned for us to go ahead while she stayed behind, already happily perusing other pattern books. Vanessa led the way to the back office, followed by

Orwin, who was eager to see what he could have missed that his hackings skills hadn't acquired. Knox fell into step beside me.

I'd give the two of you some privacy, but I wouldn't want to cause the alien hunter's allergies to get any worse.

"Are you really okay after what happened?" Knox asked softly, even leaning down a bit so that his voice didn't carry. He could whisper, but Pearl would still hear him. "I'm as disappointed as you are that Ammeline isn't still in the area, but we'll figure it out. Orwin will create an algorithm, we'll accumulate information, and then we'll figure out her plan."

"That's going to take a lot of time," I reminded him, stopping just outside the back room so that I could answer him. "We didn't even know if the proximity spell worked until today, Knox. At this rate, it's going to take years."

We all know that your patience is rather thin, dear hexed one. There are times we aren't given a choice but to dig deeper. Perhaps you'll find a way to make the time go by faster.

"It's a good thing we have people to save and justice to serve." Knox winked at me before he entered the back room. "So, what do we have?"

That wolfman is a flirtatious one, isn't he?

"I'm going to tell Piper that she needs to knit you booties for all four paws," I threatened, joining the others to see what it was we could have missed in those emails.

I do so love a challenge, dear hexed one.

"We have nothing," Orwin replied from the desk chair of Norma's desk. Vanessa, and now Knox, stood behind him. The back room was used for inventory, but Norma had cleared a corner spot for her desk and file cabinet. "There's nothing here."

"I really thought we'd find something," Vanessa said, desperation in her tone. She looked at Knox when asking her next question, but she was basically doubting our abilities. "Are you sure that Gracie Lynn is innocent?"

"Yes," I replied, having full confidence in Orwin's abilities. "All roads are leading us toward the Wilkes, but the entire misunderstanding that Edgar and Roger spoke about has that theory up in the air."

Although I have declared the compassionate couple innocent, that does not mean Mr. and Mrs. Wilkes aren't privy to some information that could help us. Perhaps it's time for our alien hunter to pay them a visit. I'll supervise, of course.

I'm sure that Pearl would travel along with Orwin for another chance at a spot of warm cream heated to perfection, and that might need to be the route we took this afternoon. Orwin and Pearl could use a cover story where an owner had lost his cat, though the Wilkes would most likely see through that façade, given that he wasn't local. Throw in a veterinarian's office and an emergency visit from a man traveling with his cat, and such a tale could be convincing with the right amount of urgency.

I admire your creativity, dear hexed one.

"Wait a second."

Orwin leaned forward on the desk chair far enough that there was a good chance it could wheel right out from under him. He pushed his black-rimmed glasses up as he studied the screen in front of him. I glanced at Knox, hoping for some sign that would explain what had caught Orwin's attention, but all Knox did was shrug in bewilderment.

"Do you see that date?" Orwin asked Vanessa, pointing to somewhere on the screen. "I've gone over your aunt and uncle's calendar the week before the murder multiple times. Norma couldn't have sent this email to Mrs. Wilkes about reneging on their verbal agreement. She wasn't in the shop that afternoon."

Speaking of admiration, I suppose some should be given to the alien hunter for his technological abilities.

"Why should that make a difference?" Knox asked, frowning at such an announcement. "I send emails from my phone all the time, so it shouldn't matter that Norma Booneville wasn't here that day."

The wolfman makes a good point, alien hunter.

"It does if Aunt Norma was somewhere that couldn't get phone reception," Vanessa replied in disbelief, lifting a hand to her mouth. "Uncle Edgar and Aunt Norma had gone to one of the ski lodges. I know for a fact that the cabin they stay in doesn't get service, and they like it that way. No Wi-Fi, either. They reserve that overnight every year to get away. It was a tradition started many years ago by my aunt, because scheduling something like that was the only way to guarantee my uncle wouldn't cancel. He loved his work."

"This was the misunderstanding," Orwin said, his dark gaze traveling up to meet mine. "Someone didn't want Debbie to become a partner. Whoever sent this email is the murderer."

We are one step closer to solving this murder mystery, and for once that app of my sweet Piper's cannot claim victory. Zero for technology, one for the human race. I sense a spot of warm cream curled up inside our traveling home in our near future.

"Wait," I exclaimed, trying to make sense of things. "Wouldn't Norma have seen the email exchange? Didn't Debbie reply with her resignation?"

"Mrs. Wilkes didn't hit reply," Orwin explained, gesturing toward the monitor once more. "She attached her resignation letter to a new email. Let me check something else."

Orwin's fingers moved over the keyboard at a rapid rate.

"Just as I thought," Orwin exclaimed in victory. "The email sent from Norma was deleted from the sent folder."

"Which only moved it into the trash file, but it was never emptied," Vanessa whispered as she tried to make sense of things.

"Going with this theory, it stands to reason that whoever sent this email found out that Mr. Booneville and Mr. Wilkes had figured out there had been a miscommunication," Orwin said, standing up from the chair in excitement. "The two men were having a meal when Gracie Lynn confronted Mr. Booneville."

It was that waitress. I told you that she was a horrible person. A la Guillotine!

"No." I'd seen firsthand how gossip traveled in small towns. As for Pearl, her mercilessness was getting out of control. "That type of confrontation would have been the news of the day, and the person who sent the email would have had access to this very computer."

True, and that waitress couldn't even work a microwave.

"Unless whoever killed Uncle Edgar had access to their house," Vanessa pointed out, but we all agreed that wasn't a likely scenario. "Who would—"

Knox's shoulders tensed as his golden gaze focused on the doorway. A quick look revealed that no one was there, but I trusted Knox with my life. I was the closest, so I quickly made my way through the doorframe.

Be careful, dear hexed one!

I quickly scanned the faces of those who were shopping inside the store, noticing that Piper was standing near the door with an alarmed expression on her face. The five other patrons had turned to see why someone was running for the exit, which just so happened to be behind Piper. Everyone who filed out of the back room behind me gave a collective gasp as to the identity of the guilty party.

Julie Kirkham.

And she was a mere two steps away from Piper, who was holding onto a couple of pattern books with three balls of yarn. It was clear that she'd hastily made the connection at seeing the panic written across the older woman's face. There was only one thing to do, and that was to stop Julie from shoving Piper to the ground in her bid to flee.

I lifted a hand, promptly causing the pattern books and yarn in Piper's hands to fly into Julie's face. The split second she put her hands up and leaned back to protect herself, I used my ability to swipe Julie's feet out from underneath her.

Nicely done, dear hexed one. No one is the wiser as to how Mrs. Kirkham tripped, but I do have to wonder if my sweet Piper is rubbing off on you. I'm not so sure I would have cushioned a murderer's fall with those three balls of yarn.

"Nice work," Knox murmured as he passed by me to make sure that Julie didn't try to make another run for it. "Orwin, would you please call those detectives?"

Orwin was already dialing 911. Piper had gone to reassure the other patrons that things were under control, and I could hear Vanessa saying her aunt's name into her cell phone. There were some lose ends to tie up, but we'd managed to bring a killer to justice.

Did you ever doubt us, dear hexed one?

"I'm the one who keeps this place together," Julie cried out in protest after Knox told her that she wasn't going anywhere until the police arrived. "Debbie didn't deserve to be partner. I did!"

Julie seemed to have realized that she'd implicated herself while in a panic, and she tried her best to backpedal her confession. Knox just crossed his arms, letting her know that nothing she did or said was going to get him to let her pass.

"You can't prove a thing," Julie exclaimed in alarm, turning around to face Vanessa. "Not a thing!"

"I do believe that purchasing mistletoe oil in bulk on the internet is sufficient evidence to tie you to Mr. Booneville's murder, Mrs. Kirkham," Orwin announced, holding up his phone. It appeared that he'd been able to access her bank account in record time. "Did you believe that both of the Boonevilles would drink the hot chocolate? Did you want to eliminate both of them?"

Julie began to sob, although we were able to make out that she hadn't wanted to kill anyone. She'd just wanted the Boonevilles to become sick long enough to give her time to figure a way out of the mess she'd gotten herself into.

This is why I always stress to my sweet Piper that the truth will always prevail.

"Good work, Orwin," I said after he'd finished talking with the 911 operator. The police were on their way, and it wouldn't be long before we were able to leave town and drive back to the campsite. "I'm not sure Julie would have been caught had you not made the connection to the date on the emails."

"This just earned me a trip to Area 51, right?" Orwin asked, pushing up his glasses as he flashed me a smile. "I've decided to send Pearl inside so that she can bring me out evidence that the site is used to secure captured alien lifeforms."

This is the first I'm hearing about this. I do believe that you need my agreement on such an endeavor, alien hunter.

The two continued to banter back and forth about Area 51, giving me time to go back over the last few days, particularly my conversation with a certain individual in a red suit. The others seemed convinced that Kris Kringle, St. Nicholas, or whatever you wanted to call Santa Claus might very well be real. I realized that bargaining never got me anywhere, but I wasn't so sure I could believe in his existence until I'd witnessed the miracle he'd talked about firsthand.

You do understand that's not how it works, dear hexed one.

"Yeah, yeah," I muttered, sticking to my stubborn ways, anyway. "Knock-knock."

I see you're turning the tables on me, Miss Lilura. Okay, I'll play. Who's there?

"Coal."

Orwin muttered something about being stuck with dimwits, but he'd done so in an affectionate manner.

Coal who?

"Coal me if you find the real Santa."

I did manage to get a chuckle out of Orwin as he

walked over to explain to Piper how we'd figured out who murdered Edgar Booneville, as well as to remind her that a stop at the post office was next up on our agenda. Sugar cookies had been sent by her father, and Orwin wasn't one to pass up homemade baked goods. Knox was still standing guard, and Vanessa was still deep in conversation with her aunt on the phone. As for me? Well, I felt pretty good having come up with that knock-knock joke all on my own. Maybe I was making progress in that silver lining department, after all.

You have a long way to go. That wasn't funny in the least, dear hexed one.

Chapter Fourteen

CHRISTMAS EVE HAD arrived with another blanket of snow. I'd had another premonition not an hour out from Covered Bridge, though that murder mystery had been relatively easy to solve. Pearl had told Orwin of my wish to spend the holiday in a remote full-service cabin that could host all of us comfortably, even though I'd prompted all of them to take these few days to go and spend it with family.

We are already among family, dear hexed one.

I wasn't going to deny that I was grateful for a reprieve. We never knew when I'd receive a premonition, so this small time we'd been able to carve out was special.

Maybe a miracle?

Piper and Orwin were putting the finishing touches on the Christmas tree that Knox had managed to procure for us, bickering about how much space to leave between the strings of popcorn.

"I wouldn't go that far," I said wryly, wiping my hands on a dishtowel. Pearl and I had made a pan of lasagna for dinner. Technically, Pearl was just overseeing the only meal I really knew how to make from scratch. "But I'll take these rare moments of peace any way I can get them."

It certainly wasn't a waste. You now know how to make polenta.

"It wasn't easy," I reminded her, rotating my wrist before reaching for my glass of eggnog. The only thing left for us to do was set the table, but dinner wouldn't be ready for another thirty minutes. I'd put Pearl's special dish in the bottom drawer of the oven to keep warm, which meant we had time to relax by the fire. "And when have you ever fancied Italian?"

I'm a familiar with many eclectic tastes, Miss Lilura.

We'd been playing Christmas music all evening, even joining in on the lyrics we knew by heart. Piper started singing along now, even grabbing one of her knitting needles to use as a microphone. She'd basically knitted nonstop since we'd left Covered Bridge, pulling up YouTube videos when she wasn't quite sure about a specific stitch. I had no doubt that the wrapped presents she'd lugged in from the RV were all knitted apparel.

I'd gone out earlier today to buy a few presents of my own to give out to the group, hoping that each personalized gift denoted how much I appreciated their friendship. I'd even bought something special for Pearl, but I'd been doing my best not to think about it in hopes to keep it a secret until tomorrow morning.

You're doing a spectacular job of it, too, though I highly doubt you can hold out until morning. No worries, dear hexed one. I have more than enough patience for us both.

There was a muffled thud that came from the front door, though Piper and Orwin couldn't hear it over the music. I'd curled up on the couch, with Pearl doing the same on the armrest, but neither of us moved from our comfortable positions. Knox was expected to return from his run any moment.

After another minute passed, Pearl and I exchanged curious and concerned glances.

Fine. Seeing as I'm more equipped to go outside, I'll go check on our resident werewolf.

I smiled my appreciation, really not wanting to move off the couch. The eggnog Orwin had made was delicious, the roaring fire had set a cozy mood, and all I wanted to do was enjoy the peace that would surely be shattered in a day or two.

It's rather odd, Miss Lilura, but there's no sign of the wolfman's return anywhere.

"Maybe it was just some snow falling off the roof," I surmised, knowing full well we were far from civilization. I also hadn't felt Ammeline's presence since the day we solved Edgar Booneville's murder, so I wasn't worried that the Lich Queen had snuck up on us. "The winds are picking up out there."

That doesn't explain the large boot prints in front of the door, nor why there are no receding tracks other than what is under the dusting of snow we've received since Mr. Emeric went for his nightly run.

"Maybe they are Knox's boot prints, and the fresh

snow just didn't reach the area underneath the over-hang," I proposed, already knowing from Pearl's narrowed green eyes that I was going to have to unravel myself from the couch. "Fine, I'll go have a look."

I was wearing fuzzy socks that I'd bought while on my shopping spree, a little gift to me for the holidays. In order for them not to get wet, I made sure to stand just inside the doorframe after I'd swung open the front door. Sure enough, there were two boot prints facing the door.

How do you suppose they got there, dear hexed one?

I continued to hold my eggnog while scanning the area that the porch light could reach. Beyond that was darkness. The flurries had now turned to big, fat snowflakes that added to the inches already on the ground. I followed their path, noticing that they were just now covering the fresh boot prints in front of me. Before I could call out to Orwin and Piper to come take a look and give me their opinion, I heard rustling coming from the tree line.

"Everything okay?" Knox called out, emerging from the darkness. He hadn't bothered to wear a jacket. He must have tucked his clothes somewhere safe to remain dry, though his black hair was a bit wet from his run. "Why are you standing there in the cold?"

"Pearl and I thought we heard something," I replied, looking back down so that I could show Knox what we'd discovered, only the prints had now been filled with fresh snow. Impossible. "Knox, there were two boot prints here. I swear."

I met Knox's gaze, so richly gold in color, only to find him flashing me that crooked smile of his. His gaze went above my head, so I instinctively followed his amusing stare.

Is that…mistletoe?

"All you had to do was ask, Lou."

By the time my brain registered that I was standing underneath mistletoe, Knox had taken a step forward. His warm hand cradled my face as he leaned down, his soft lips pressing against mine.

Time stood still.

When Knox finally pulled away, I heard…

Ringing bells and a rich *ho-ho-ho* that faded into the night sky.

I do believe St. Nicholas kept his word on giving you an early Christmas present, Miss Lilura. We know that magic is real, so it stands to reason that so are miracles. Merry Christmas, dear hexed one.

~ THE END ~

It's a bait and switch whodunit in the next installment of the Hex on Me Mysteries by USA Today Bestselling Author Kennedy Layne…

kennedylayne.com/curse-me-under-the-mistletoe.html

Creating beautiful snow angels, cross-country skiing for miles, and riding toboggans over snowy hills are all exciting outdoor activities to do in the winter months. When Lou's latest premonition of murder takes her and the gang to an isolated ice fishing shack in the middle of a lake in the upper peninsula of Michigan, it looks as if they're about to go fishing for a murderer.

You'll want to bring along a seat warmer and an ice fishing pole for this mystery if you want to help Lou and the gang hook a whale of a killer!

Books by Kennedy Layne

Hex on Me Mysteries
If the Curse Fits
Cursing up the Wrong Tree
The Squeaky Ghost Gets the Curse
The Curse that Bites
Curse Me Under the Mistletoe

Paramour Bay Mysteries
Magical Blend
Bewitching Blend
Enchanting Blend
Haunting Blend
Charming Blend
Spellbinding Blend
Cryptic Blend
Broomstick Blend
Spirited Blend
Yuletide Blend

Office Roulette Series
Means (Office Roulette, Book One)
Motive (Office Roulette, Book Two)
Opportunity (Office Roulette, Book Three)

Keys to Love Series
Unlocking Fear (Keys to Love, Book One)
Unlocking Secrets (Keys to Love, Book Two)
Unlocking Lies (Keys to Love, Book Three)
Unlocking Shadows (Keys to Love, Book Four)
Unlocking Darkness (Keys to Love, Book Five)

SURVIVING ASHES SERIES
Essential Beginnings (Surviving Ashes, Book One)
Hidden Ashes (Surviving Ashes, Book Two)
Buried Flames (Surviving Ashes, Book Three)
Endless Flames (Surviving Ashes, Book Four)
Rising Flames (Surviving Ashes, Book Five)

CSA CASE FILES SERIES
Captured Innocence (CSA Case Files 1)
Sinful Resurrection (CSA Case Files 2)
Renewed Faith (CSA Case Files 3)
Campaign of Desire (CSA Case Files 4)
Internal Temptation (CSA Case Files 5)
Radiant Surrender (CSA Case Files 6)
Redeem My Heart (CSA Case Files 7)
A Mission of Love (CSA Case Files 8)

RED STARR SERIES
Starr's Awakening(Red Starr, Book One)
Hearths of Fire (Red Starr, Book Two)
Targets Entangled (Red Starr, Book Three)
Igniting Passion (Red Starr, Book Four)
Untold Devotion (Red Starr, Book Five)
Fulfilling Promises (Red Starr, Book Six)
Fated Identity (Red Starr, Book Seven)
Red's Salvation (Red Starr, Book Eight)

THE SAFEGUARD SERIES
Brutal Obsession (The Safeguard Series, Book One)
Faithful Addiction (The Safeguard Series, Book Two)
Distant Illusions (The Safeguard Series, Book Three)
Casual Impressions (The Safeguard Series, Book Four)
Honest Intentions (The Safeguard Series, Book Five)
Deadly Premonitions (The Safeguard Series, Book Six)

About the Author

First and foremost, I love life. I love that I'm a wife, mother, daughter, sister… and a writer.

I am one of the lucky women in this world who gets to do what makes them happy. As long as I have a cup of coffee (maybe two or three) and my laptop, the stories evolve themselves and I try to do them justice. I draw my inspiration from a retired Marine Master Sergeant that swept me off of my feet and has drawn me into a world that fulfills all of my deepest and darkest desires. Erotic romance, military men, intrigue, with a little bit of kinky chili pepper (his recipe), fill my head and there is nothing more satisfying than making the hero and heroine fulfill their destinies.

Thank you for having joined me on their journeys…

Email:

kennedylayneauthor@gmail.com

Facebook:

facebook.com/kennedy.layne.94

Twitter:

twitter.com/KennedyL_Author

Website:

www.kennedylayne.com

Newsletter:

www.kennedylayne.com/aboutnewsletter.html